PENGUIN BOOKS
LIKE MEN BETR

John Mortimer is a playw͟ ͟ ͟ ͟ ͟ ͟ ͟ ͟ ͟ ͟ ͟ ͟ ͟ ͟ prac-
tising barrister. During the war he worked with the Crown
Film Unit and published a number of novels before turning
to the theatre with such plays as *The Dock Brief*, *The Wrong
Side of the Park* and *A Voyage Round My Father*. He has written
many film scripts, radio plays and television plays, including
six plays on the life of Shakespeare, the Rumpole plays,
which won him the British Academy Writer of the Year
Award, and the adaptation of Evelyn Waugh's *Brideshead
Revisited*. His translations of Feydeau have been performed at
the National Theatre and are published in Penguin as *Three
Boulevard Farces*. Penguin publish his collections of stories
Rumpole of the Bailey, *The Trials of Rumpole*, *Rumpole's Return*,
Rumpole for the Defence, *Rumpole and the Golden Thread* and
Rumpole's Last Case as well as *The First Rumpole Omnibus* and
The Second Rumpole Omnibus. Also published in Penguin are
two volumes of John Mortimer's plays; his acclaimed auto-
biography *Clinging to the Wreckage*, which won the *Yorkshire
Post* Book of the Year Award; *In Character* and *Character Parts*,
which contain interviews with some of the most famous
men and women of our time; *Charade*, his first novel; and
Paradise Postponed, which was made into a major television
drama series. John Mortimer lives with his wife and their
two daughters in what was once his father's house in the
Chilterns.

JOHN MORTIMER

Like Men Betrayed

PENGUIN BOOKS

PENGUIN BOOKS

Published by the Penguin Group
27 Wrights Lane, London w8 5TZ, England
Viking Penguin Inc., 40 West 23rd Street, New York, New York 10010, USA
Penguin Books Australia Ltd, Ringwood, Victoria, Australia
Penguin Books Canada Ltd, 2801 John Street, Markham, Ontario, Canada L3R 1B4
Penguin Books (NZ) Ltd, 182–190 Wairau Road, Auckland 10, New Zealand

Penguin Books Ltd, Registered Offices: Harmondsworth, Middlesex, England

First published by Collins 1953
Published in Penguin Books 1988

Copyright © 1953 by Advanpress Ltd
All rights reserved

Made and printed in Great Britain by
Hazell Watson & Viney Limited
Member of BPCC plc
Aylesbury, Bucks, England
Filmset in Bembo

For
Penelope Mortimer

Action is transitory, a step, a blow,
The motion of a muscle – this way or that
'Tis done, and in the after vacancy
We wonder at ourselves like men betrayed . . .

WILLIAM WORDSWORTH

Contents

I

People in Pairs

Two men faced each other across the club table, the one cheerfully insensitive to the other's well-restrained dislike.

'Queer sorts of joints, these clubs,' Porcher, the new member was saying. 'Of course, now I'm in the Ministry, they come in useful for lunching a friend from time to time. Impresses some people – I don't know why.'

Kennet curled a large hand round his club size port and looked up at the obstinate, rakish features of Lord Palmerston over the mantelpiece. Crammed into furniture seemingly selected at random from station waiting-rooms, his club had never seemed to him a particularly impressive place. It was simply the place where, for the last twenty-five years, he had enjoyed having his lunch.

'You solicitor blokes have to lunch the important client from time to time too, eh? Lots of business done over the tablecloth these days.'

'No, I've never bought a client a meal. I come here to stop them pestering me.'

'Is that so? Mind you, for homely fun the old Barnsley Radical Club took a lot of beating. In my town council days we used to get four or five of us bright lads in there of a lunch time. There was a waitress there, a bright lass if ever there was one . . .'

Porcher bit on a curly pipe and fumbled across his distended waistcoat for matches. He spoke with a Yorkshire accent which became more pronounced every year with his rise to political power. As a young man his voice had been urban and refined, now that he was middle-aged and a Junior Minister he assumed the role of a North Country farm labourer. His voice was meant to drift comfortingly across the wireless waves, recalling dumplings, Yorkshire pudding and low comics. In deference to the cartoonists he had arranged his scant hair in a modest forelock.

'Ay bright lads we were. Now my old friend from those days, Arthur Harris, he's on the electricity board and I've scraped myself into the Government, so we have to be more careful. No good popping round the corner to the A.B.C. as I've done many a time and oft in the last parliament. When in Rome you know . . .'

Kennet shifted in his chair and looked hopelessly at the man opposite. He felt like an insular traveller who has been drawn into an intimate conversation in a language of which he has no command.

'Careful. That's what you've got to be. Use the office car for a jaunt or go for a bit of homely fun up the West End and the newspapers come down on you like a cat on hot bricks.' The mixing of metaphors had long been a reassuring facet of Porcher's speeches. 'Some lads, lads I've known well too, sniff of office goes to their heads like a win on the pools. Then it's nothing for them but the Savoy and holidays in Bournemouth. There's nothing like that about my family. Quiet livers we are. Very quiet livers.'

'Bournemouth,' the pause had been so long Kennet felt that something was expected of him. 'A place I've never much enjoyed.'

'It's the same with you lot, I suppose.'

'With us?'

'Ay, solicitors.' Porcher had lit his pipe and his beady eyes shone at Kennet through the smoke.

'I don't quite see . . .'

'Temptations. Position of trust. Might have a bad effect on some people. Corrupting if you take what I mean.'

Lunch time had always been for Kennet a quiet, almost a hallowed time. He went to his club rather as the devout, passing through a hot city square, slip into a cathedral to sit in the shadows and contemplate. The time was an oasis in his day. Nothing so pleasant, he would have said had he ever troubled to formulate the exact values of his existence, awaited him at home after his work was finished. He was startled, therefore, by the sudden feat of mental gymnastics required of him by this twist in the conversation. It was as if the devotee in the cathedral had been required, by a passing priest, to solve an acrostic.

'I don't really see . . .'

'Oh come now. There've been one or two cases recently, and a few more, I should think, who've been clever enough not to be caught out. Jobs like ours, they've got risks attached, that's the only point I'm bringing out.'

Faced with it Kennet considered the situation.

'I can't say I've ever felt inclined to hang on to my clients' money. It'd be much more trouble, I'd fancy, than it would be worth in the long run.'

'Of course we realize that.' Porcher took his bill and stood up. 'How's your boy these days?'

'My boy? Oh Kit. He's well I think. I didn't know you knew him.'

'Yes. We meet now and then. He gets about. Doing well isn't he?'

'I hardly know,' Kennet was puzzled. 'He's certainly given up asking me for money.'

Loud and humourless as the applause of a wireless audience, Porcher's laughter echoed through the room.

'I'll bet he has. Go far that boy of yours will. He's got his head screwed on they say where I come from. Going to be a member here is he?'

'I don't know. He's never suggested it.'

'Ripe lad that. Go far. Well, good-day to you.'

The lunch room was emptying and Kennet, still nursing his port, was left alone with Lord Palmerston. For some reason Porcher's mention of his son Kit had disturbed him, started a train of thought which he found unsettling and unpleasant. He could not imagine how Kit had come to know Porcher, or what there was in his son for Porcher to admire. The thought of his parenthood gave him a glimpse of a chain of future events, springing from himself, which he would have no power to control or understand.

When a waiter told him that he was wanted on the telephone he felt he had half expected the call. He finished his wine and walked heavily down the passage to the dark telephone booth.

It was his office. The voice of his managing clerk sounded puzzled and respectful.

'There's a gentleman been in, sir. He'll be back at three o'clock. It's in connection with the Monument Trusts. I've been going through it and there are one or two things I can't quite straight with him, sir. I told him you'd be back, was that right?'

'Quite right. Yes. I'll be back.'

'He was inquiring about Mr Kit at first, sir, but I didn't know where he was.'

'Kit. Did you say he wanted Kit?'

'Yes sir.'

'Very well. I'll come straight back.'

Kennet came down the steps into the street and it was raining, soft rain which hit the pavement without a sound. As he stopped to get into a cab he felt a sinking in his stomach, like a man who has been free but on bail, and is at last being driven to his trial.

Behind him his acquaintances in the club windows said, 'There goes Kennet. Still carrying on you know. But none of us get any younger.'

In the Urquharts' room the atmosphere was one of extreme torpor. The two figures in it sat immobile, the signs of their existence, the open cigarette carton, the remains of supper, the baby's nappy on the corner of the sofa, were like the unexpected clues to a lost civilization caught and preserved beneath the molten lava of a past eruption. And yet, Sylvia

Urquhart thought, nothing has erupted here, nor, in all probability, ever will. She sat on the floor in front of the electric fire. The dry metallic heat made her head throb. She gazed at the newspaper on the floor which she had already read twice. She sniffed cautiously, smelling on herself the moist, milky smell of the baby which was asleep in their only other room. She was new to the smell, which had descended on her recently and for the first time. It made her feel unapproachable and alone.

Her husband sat at the table and looked at an empty piece of paper in his typewriter. He had been looking at it for a very long time. He appeared completely exhausted as if its blankness had sucked away all his energy and blotted out all his thought. Locked away inside him, no doubt, was a demon anxious to burst into song, rampage round the room or cover the paper with a confusion of dazzling words. Nothing could happen, however, while the body sat inert, hypnotized by the white glare of the paper.

He's like, Sylvia thought, the baby sucking at the nipple. The expression of concentrated vacancy is the same. No one could call it happiness. And I'm like him. I give suck, and when I'm dry I sit here watching him, pretending to read the *Evening Standard*. Nervously she thought that one day her baby would have to be weaned, or her husband might even succeed in finishing a chapter.

He picked up a pencil now and sharpened it with a blunt penknife. Slivers of wood fell on to the carpet. The point broke and he swore gently. Then he started sharpening again. Good, she thought, he'll be glad of the exercise.

Above them the tall house, which they had bought when they couldn't afford it and now let off to various lodgers, talked like a sailing ship in a high wind. How happy we are, Sylvia thought, now that the lodgers have forced us down to the basement and we no longer have the responsibility for all those rooms. Besides the lodgers were so amusing, having them in the background gave, almost, the illusion that life was going on around you.

Sylvia stroked her thighs and thought about her lodgers. The newspaper she had just read she found meaningless, a confused jumble of sentences. Remote from her, in the outside world, troops were moving, film stars were dying and boxers were knocking each other out. Of this scarcely a thud reverberated in the basement of 9 Godiva Crescent. The clank of the chain, however, as the Indian student came out of the lavatory, the creak of the stairboard as the commercial artist hurried upstairs with his girlfriend, the tattoo as the medical student knocked out his enormous pipe: to all these sounds she was sensitive. They gave her, in their separate ways, deep pleasure. She liked to think of people immersed in hot water, or locked in warm lavatories, or slipping, without undue effort, into the quiescence of love. And as she was staring contentedly in front of her, footsteps came down the stairs and paused before the door.

The penknife poised over the pencil. The Urquharts looked at each other without breathing. Someone was coming in.

But the footsteps resumed and the door remained shut. Under it, however, had appeared the white corner of an envelope. The front door banged. They both looked at the envelope as if it might explode.

At last the man approached it, picked it up and opened it with his penknife. In it he found a typewritten note and a cheque.

'Young Kit Kennet,' he said. 'Doesn't know when he'll be back. He wants to keep on the room though, and here's a month's rent in advance.'

He held out the cheque distastefully, as if he found such ready payment in bad taste.

'But why . . .' his wife sighed, 'not come in and say good-bye – and why all that at once and . . . and where can he find to go to – at this time of night?'

'I can't understand Kennet. I never have understood him.' Urquhart sounded resentful as if, for some reason, he expected to understand most things.

★

The fat man said to the girl, 'Waiting for Kit Kennet?'

The girl was very young. She looked up at him with contempt from the café table at which she sat. In front of her was a cup of coffee which she didn't drink, and a little pile of money ready to pay for the coffee.

She said, 'Oh, go away, Seton. He doesn't like you. He won't come if you're here.'

'Not like me? Why wouldn't Kit Kennet like me?' The fat man sank plaintively into the chair opposite her, looking and sounding like a partially deflated balloon floating sadly to earth. 'Do you know what the time is?'

The question seemed to take the girl aback. She looked round her hopelessly, as if trying to deduce the passage of time from the greasiness of the food, the muddiness of the coffee and the weariness of the customers.

The fat man, who was a poet named Seton, continued to look at her with the small, wretched eyes of a lap dog on whom a heavy woman has just sat by mistake.

'Anna darling,' he said, 'it must be past eleven.'

'Well?'

'It's late for Kit Kennet.'

'He's sometimes late.'

A tattooed Greek passed them with two plates of fish and chips. The fish was encased in a great balloon of batter and looked as if it had been blown up with a bicycle pump. Seton looked at the food wistfully; the girl as if it were a nasty accident being carried by on a stretcher.

Seton asked, 'Do you want to eat?'

'Of course not.'

There was a silence. Suddenly Seton began to intone, in a high-pitched, carefully unctuous voice, *'For all the nightmares I am worthy of,/I wrap and post to my brown paper love.* Do you know what that means, Anna?'

'No.'

'It's a poem I wrote ten years ago. Buggered if I can remember what about. Do you like poetry at all?'

'No.' She was craning round his huge bulk to see the door.

'That's him,' she said as a figure in a dark overcoat came down the stairs, looked round and went out again.

'No, it's not,' Seton said. He drew on a minute cigarette which stuck in his mouth as if put there to mark the opening. 'God, to have the dear war back,' he said. 'All the girls liked poetry then, and poets. The pickups! Fabulous, I tell you. It was a sparse, spring morning when the typists were sprouting like daffodils out of Green Park tube station and I was heaving this weight of carrion up the escalator . . .'

He clasped his hands to his stomach, his little mouth carefully circled the long, stilted phrases. His eyes were wet with genuine feeling, nostalgia for the silvery barrage balloons in the blue sky, the humming canteen of the Ministry of Information, and his archetype in green trousers with shoulder-length hair and a new copy of *Horizon*.

'I'd been to a party and slept the night on a kitchen table. I knew I looked sinister, like an unfrocked parson or a spy gone fat in a neutral country . . .'

The girl looked at him, her eyes wide. She was neither censorious nor interested. She said, 'Do go away.'

Unabashed, the fat man continued. 'I was wearing that overcoat of mine – you know, the black one. And a curious pair of red gloves I'd picked up by mistake in the B.B.C. A shady surgeon, I suppose, I might even have been.'

'If you will stay,' said the girl, 'keep quiet.'

'And a frightful little hat, like a child's paper boat. . . . Am I boring you?'

She didn't answer, still gazing at the door.

The café was beginning to fill up. It was one of those cafés, originally the meeting place of cab drivers and Cypriot waiters, which had become, temporarily, haunted by people of all classes who found themselves out at night. When the pubs closed and the theatres finished they came crowding in, whores with pale, moon faces and tow-coloured hair, ballet girls with blue-lidded eyes and cockney accents, students in glasses and great mufflers, pimps and pansies with coffee-coloured shirts and hand-painted ties. They packed the restaurant out, moved the chairs, rearranged the tables, borrowed money, kissed each other and sat on each other's laps. The Greek proprietor, who seemed to hate them indiscriminately, swore at them, occasionally struck them, forgot or confused their orders. The girl, unblinking and aloof, stared across them at the door.

'What does interest you?' Seton was asking. 'Kit Kennet? Ah, but he fascinates me. He's a monster, of course. They say so. The most extraordinary young man possible to imagine. Do you know, Anna, he's always making money?'

'Is he?'

At the next table, a thin man, who kept his hat on, had ordered a cup of coffee. He took out a tin and started to roll a cigarette as he listened to Seton. He was watching him, too, with one eye, the other sightless and stationary.

'Parson Dobson told me a story,' Seton said. 'You know Parson, a Jew, of course, and a liar, and one of the biggest pimps in London, but a dear friend of mine. You know his pictures, too – brilliant, hilarious. Victorian Welsh chapels by moonlight. Parson knew Kit when he was still at school. Said he was a beautiful bone-shaped boy, reminded him of some acolyte he once met in Birmingham. At any rate, Kit told Parson how much he liked his painting. So Parson gave him a picture one Christmas, he thought it would be a thing Kit would treasure all his life. But here's the horror of it. Do you know what Kit did the day after Boxing Day?'

'Sold it.' She had heard it before.

'Yes!' Seton nodded and wriggled with delighted horror. 'Of course Parson was fascinated to know what he'd done with the money – I mean, one could have u[...] he'd run off with a girl or something. But [...] thing he bought –' He paused. She was rearr[...] of coins on the table, hardly listening. The r[...]

19

table moved his cigarette from one corner of his mouth to the other and lit it, bending his head forward to hear the end of Seton's story.

'He bought rubber shares. Can you imagine? He sold Parson's picture to buy rubber. I believe it went up enormously.' He leant back in his chair, his story triumphantly concluded. The man at the next table did not smile.

'He's not like us, Anna.' Seton leant forward again sadly. 'He's different from us. Now would you do that? Would I? We'd never think of it.'

The girl was silent. The café was closing, the proprietor was going among the tables collecting dirty plates and asking his customers if they had no homes.

'He won't come now,' Seton said. 'We'd better go.'

'All right.'

The man at the next table snapped his tin of tobacco shut, paid for his coffee and left before them.

Seton and the girl climbed the steps up to the street together. A fine rain was sifting down on Charlotte Street and Seton pulled on a very small check cap.

'What will happen to a person like Kit, what can happen to him?' Seton was saying. 'That's what one asks oneself. What can possibly be the end of him? Did I tell you I know his family?'

'No,' the girl answered.

'His mother best. One of my patronesses, dear. A delightful, cultivated woman – a little icy if you understand me, but a very cultivated woman. And his father –'

The girl looked up at him through the rain, almost, for a moment, interested. 'What's his father like?'

'Oh, very ordinary, I think you'd find. Not like us either. A martyr, almost, to his ordinariness. Where are you going to sleep?'

'I don't know yet.'

'Extraordinary you are. Don't you live anywhere?'

The girl looked at him disdainfully, her face wet. 'where particular just now.'

'Then you'd better come home with me. I've got a mattress.'

She did not thank him, or make any comment, but she allowed him to take her home to his flat. The tearful, fat, affected man fussed over her solicitously, found an army blanket and extra pillows, made her tea which she drank thirstily. He unrolled the mattress which had accommodated so many drunks, American sailors, film directors and vicars' daughters. Then he watered his cactus, fed his cat and undressed.

Before he went to bed he came in to say goodnight. The girl had fallen asleep with the naked electric light bulb still burning. He stood in the doorway in crumpled mauve pyjamas, smoking a Woodbine, feeling lonely and oppressed. She was so young and exhausted and seemed, like a missionary or a nursing sister, dedicated, infamously chaste.

2

People Alone

Far out of London, too far for the stockbrokers, popular novelists or matinée idols to find cottages, so far that a man would only go there to retire or die, at the end of a journey entailing changes at two bleak and clangorous railway junctions, lay the village of Worsfold. Inaccessible, high, remote, it preserved, almost intact, every discomfort of the English way of life as lived during the closing years of the last century.

Over the surrounding country illiteracy and incest were on the way out, the status of women had, if only imperceptibly, been raised, drunkenness and suicide declined. Worsfold, with its thick-walled stone cottages and its impossible roads was unchanged. There was not a door in Worsfold that fitted, and the wind came usually from the east; there was not a boiler in Worsfold that worked, and the bath water stemmed from a metallic quarry which made it dark brown as well as cold. Mains electricity, sanitation, water, to these the inhabitants of Worsfold were strangers. They manufactured their light with rejected American Army engines, mechanisms which only performed reliably in the summer months. They cooked sporadically with gas brought in large cylinders of sinister appearance which often leaked, giving the inside of cottages the smell of a dentist's surgery.

In the teeth of so much opposition from nature the country gentlemen of the district continued, however, to live lives of pleasure. Men hunted there, three times a week, while their women tried to light, with blue fingers, paraffin lamps in stone flagged kitchens. Horses received hot mash in the evenings while young wives in gumboots struggled, ineffectually, to open a tin of sardines. In Worsfold women early lost their looks, their clothes degenerated, their hopes disappeared as they stood in out-houses stirring chicken food. The men became lean and scrawny, their moustaches grew like untrained hedges, their overdrafts rose as they bought loads of feeding stuff or joined another hunt. Only the horses, sleek, fat, every day meticulously groomed by long-legged, pale faced children with matted hair and dusty velvet caps, only the horses undeniably prospered.

The country has been pushed together, in most corners of England a cosiness prevails, a feeling that if the situation becomes too desperate, if the fires smoke too abominably or the paraffin stoves really refuse to light, then a bus will soon be passing for the nearest town. Only in a few places today does the real isolation persist, that isolation in which the boredom can be felt hanging over the flat, uninteresting country like a mist, in which an hysterical woman might stand in the middle of a field and scream, you feel, for an hour at a time, complaining endlessly of the lack of society, lack of comfort, lack of love, with no one to hear until at last, worn out with her protest, she returns in resignation to feed the chickens.

Worsfold was such a place. In it you felt isolated as on a steppe or prairie, at a period when mud, dust and ruts constantly defeated the stage coach to the town. No rambler ever rambled to Worsfold in search of a day's pleasure, no townsman ever drove there for a picnic lunch, no one, under any circumstances, ever went there for a honeymoon. It was country to be used as country, a place in which to raise horses, poultry, cows, vegetables and children, a good place for building old fowl runs out of worn out baby Austins, a marvellous place for making little sheds out of dirty petrol cans. In fact, if you were lucky enough to be born there, it was a very good place not to die in.

But as, on the barest rock, some form of grey, lichenous life will take root, even spread, so around Worsfold the country families insisted on mating, multiplying and even falling in love and became, as their original numbers were limited, in various intricate ways, nearly all cousins. As they did so their names became grossly hyphenated and their means extremely straitened. Sons were produced who had to be sent to minor public schools, and who then expected to settle down to the traditional four days a week hunting; daughters had to be given some semblance of education before they turned their hands to breeding spaniels or raising Rhode Island Reds. Black as the immediate future seemed, however, they had expectations, and the expectations centred on their senior, widowed, unpredictable cousin, Hester Hume-Monument.

For it could be said of Worsfold, totally undistinguished as it was, with its pub and its church similar but for the addition of a stunted tower to one, an unpictorial sign to the other, that it was presided over by two remarkable deities, the sky and Mrs Hume-Monument. Of the sky, so flat and high was the place, there was a great deal, it arranged a perpetual, theatrical pageant of grey, green and crimson cloud and frequently shot rain and hail at the unappreciative village. Mrs Hume-Monument, on the other hand, was small and, apart from her scarlet gash of lipstick, colourless. Nothing which happened in the village, however, escaped her. She saw it all from her bedroom window.

She sat now, upright in bed, holding a glass of colourless fluid which a casual visitor might have supposed to have been water. As she never received casual visitors and as anyone with the slightest knowledge of her habits would have easily identified it as gin, she deceived no one. On her lap was an Air Force officer's cap which contained her patience cards, her cigarette case and lighter, both with their Air Force crests, her bobbins of silk and her piece of undistinguished petit point. Her attention, now, was divided between two men, one of whom was alive and the other dead – these were her son and her cousin Rolley, and from the point of view of their interest to Mrs Hume-Monument, or indeed to anyone else, their descriptions might have been reversed. Rolley, on horseback in the street below, unremarkable from the top of his green, pork-pie hat, a hat which made Mrs Hume-Monument choke indignantly over her gin, to the tip of his inoffensive, square-toed Army and Navy store riding boots, had a glassy, uninspired look and his moustache grew on him in the manner of unchecked post-mortem hair. For an instant he was galvanized into motion as his slowly trotting horse, seeing a sinisterly limp, grotesquely empty cement bag by Mrs Monument's front gate, shied and threw him heavily forward on to its neck and then jolted him back into the saddle. Rolley remained expressionless as a dead man, who, lashed insecurely to his horse, has been sent by some ingenious commander, long having run out of live troops, to deceive the besieging, witless Indians into thinking that help for the garrison is at hand.

His cousin, however, was diverted by the display of indifferent horsemanship. As that blinding, theatrical sky appeared between Rolley's legs she raised her glass to the postcard on the wall.

'Down the hatch, Gerry,' she said. 'Here's to the good old Duke.'

Gerry Monument, who was, in fact, dead, grinned back glossily, superficially, without real merriment, as he had in life. His portrait, like himself, was a little larger than life size. It was executed with every possible vulgarity and caught, to an amazing degree, the personality of the sitter. It was done in some contemptible medium, neither oil paint nor chalk but some mixture of crayon and tempera which allowed for glinting highlights on the short curled hair, blue reflections in the still childish eyes, greenish shadows under the square, cleft chin. Gerry was dead, but his personality filled the room and the street below, just as if his red sports car were still snorting through the village, his shaving lotion still stood in the bathroom, his filled brandy flask on the table by his bed. His face returned his mother's doting gaze, his lip curled.

'Down the hatch. His mother's a chap's best popsie.'

Gerry had actually said that to her, one morning in this very room, whilst the engine of his car ran down below and she wrote him out a cheque. By an effort of will Mrs Monument obliterated from her memory the girl who had stayed the week-end, who was waiting for Gerry in the car, and the furtive opening and shutting of bedroom doors which she had tried not to hear during the night.

She heard a tentative movement downstairs now as Rolley looked round the sitting-room, coughed in the hall. She called him up and lit a fresh cigarette from the stub of her old one. Rolley sidled into the room crab-like, shy. She remembered the confidence with which Gerry could enter any woman's bedroom, particularly his mother's.

'Hester – I was just riding by.'

'Yes, I saw you "riding".' She coughed the inverted commas round the word as she drew on her cigarette.

'I thought I'd drop in. There were one or two things –'

'Go downstairs and get a drink. You'll find youself a bottle of beer – and I'll have a gin. You know how I like it. Just up to the pretties.'

It was an aimless ruse of Mrs Monument's to send her guests downstairs to fetch her a drink although the private bottle on the floor beside her bed was still unfinished.

When Rolley returned with the drinks he sat a little behind her, spoke into her ear. Mrs Monument patted her pillows and gazed up at Gerry. Gerry looked casually down on them both.

'Here's to Gerry,' she said. 'Down the hatch.'

'Fine chap.' Rolley said so because Gerry was dead, in fact he had never liked him. 'And how are we feeling, Aunt Hester?'

'Bored.'

Rolley looked startled, as if it shocked him that anyone

should have expected to be entertained. From outside the window there came a whiff of music, the back door of the pub opposite opened and released the sound. A girl stood with her back to the lighted kitchen and emptied a basin of water out over the cabbage stalks. The low evening light dealt gently with the bare tops of her arms, the soapy water cascaded.

'Alice Crawl,' the woman in the bed muttered. 'She always does that at half-past six. I suppose it's washing up the high tea.'

'Doesn't their wireless annoy you, Aunt Hester?'

Mrs Monument wasn't listening. The sight of the girl, who now disappeared into the kitchen, gave her a curious frightened feeling, a stirring almost of sensuality. Day after day she watched Alice wash up, cut vegetables, bring in coal. She was entranced, filled with pity for the young body that lingered listlessly outside the door before turning resignedly inside. She felt sure, although she had no particular grounds for thinking it, that her son Gerry had seduced Alice Crawl. Curiously enough she wasn't jealous, as she had always been of girls whom he might have married, but the thought gave her satisfaction both warm and bitter, as if in watching carefully she could see her son's life continuing. By daily, careful observation she felt, too, that she had got inside the girl's moods, she could feel her boredom and despair, both yawned together at the narrow village, the vast, vapouring sky. They had never spoken to each other.

'Peggy wished she could have got down to see you, Aunt, only she was dog-tired. Damon's had a bit of cough – she's been sitting up with him lately.'

Rolley was burbling on. She interrupted her thoughts to say, 'Damon's the . . .?'

'Two-year-old.'

'Horse or child?'

'Oh, horse . . .' He laughed raucously.

Horse. It would have been, naturally.

What she ached for, with all the longing of her broken, emaciated body, was, at third, fourth or even fifth hand to be young again. Slowly, luxuriously, she finished her drink. When Gerry had been alive she had, in a way, kept up with the young, sitting in the back of his sports car, her thin hair dishevelled by the wind, her mouth gulping at the bludgeoning air, she had always followed the party at a safe distance. Now there was nothing left to follow, nothing left to get up for. Of the life she had had in common with the girl opposite only the dregs were left. She came out of her trance to hear Rolley asking her for something.

'So do you think, Aunt, you might possibly . . .'

'Might possibly,' she blinked, startled back to her own fifty-five years. 'Might possibly what?'

The request had obviously cost Rolley a good deal of courage to make once. He was still scarlet and shining with embarrassment, his lips were still drawn back in a humourless, ingratiating grin. The thought that all his persistence had gone for nothing, that his pleading had fallen on deaf ears, unnerved him. He could only approach his subject again indirectly.

'Well, as I was saying, a small riding school. There's room here for a small riding school, Peggy and I thought.'

'No doubt of it.'

'Good for the children.'

'Oh, the children, they can ride beautifully already. At least the girls can, up to fourteen. Then they get frightened and begin to think of getting married, have you noticed that, Rolley?'

'Peggy's still a fine horsewoman,' said Rolley, who never noticed anything in particular about people.

'Gerry was never fond of horses. I never wanted him to hunt and I remember one of his letters from Oxford . . . all about breaking in a new mare. I was terrified he was doing something dangerous, but, as it turned out, he wasn't talking about horses at all.'

'The trouble is now, the price of feeding stuffs. We should

have to have a girl to help, but she wouldn't cost much. Then there'd be advertisements, printed cards. We've got the stabling and Richard and Sue are both quiet hacks, go anywhere on the roads. Anyway, Aunt Hester, do you think it's a good scheme?'

He was standing up now, facing her. She rolled her head towards him, looking at him for the first time. Her eyes were infinitely weary, not unkind.

'No.'

He looked at the end of his boot. His mouth went down at the corners like a disappointed child's.

'Why not?'

'Because you've got no touch with money, Rolley. Some people haven't. Once you started a business like that, kept books, tried to show a profit, it'd all go – every penny you had would run from you.'

'Why can't you give us a chance, Aunt Hester? We know that you've arranged for something to come to Peggy in . . .' he blushed furiously, 'in the end. We're only asking for an advance. Five hundred would get us going, say a thousand for a real flying start.'

Her eyes went back to the portrait.

'I don't know, Rolley. I really don't know how I stand. I'll have to write to Kennet about it, take his advice.'

Rolley bit his underlip and frowned. 'All right, Aunt Hester. I'm sure old Kennet will see it's a good investment. We'll pay you interest of course. So long . . .' He frowned again. 'So long as young Kennet doesn't come into it.'

Young, had he said young? The word burst for her like an explosion in the darkening room, lighting up Gerry's portrait with a thousand coloured sparks.

'I'll write, Rolley. And I'll think about it. I promise you I will. Of course I want to help Peggy. Now go, will you? Thank you for calling in. I'm a little tired, dear, now.'

'Of course, Aunt Hester. Thank you. Of course.'

Rolley took the hand she held out for him and walked away down the stairs. He had not quite understood whether his visit had or had not been unsuccessful, and the uncertainty made him angry. Drunken old bitch, why couldn't she ever make up her mind? He mounted his horse and his irritation gave him life as he jabbed his heels into the animal's belly. At the same time he held the horse's mouth and its lip curled protestingly back on its yellow teeth. Then Rolley smiled. He wouldn't always have to go to his aunt with his cap in his hand like a schoolboy asking for pocket money; the old girl couldn't, after all, go on like it for ever. He loosened his hold on the horse's mouth and the animal gradually stopped shivering and subsided into a peaceful walk.

With curtains of green and purple and gunmetal grey, night closed the sky over Worsfold.

Hester Hume-Monument slept.

It was six o'clock in the morning when Kennet went home for a bath. A good time of the day for coughing hard and spitting on the floors of trams, a fine time for lighting the gas and slowly, resentfully, making your wife a cup of tea. It was the time when charwomen in bedroom slippers emptied office ashtrays and insomniacs drifted into their first sleep. To Kennet it seemed the time when a man over fifty should be unconscious, dead out, numb.

He opened his front door and went into his hall stooping. He was like a big man at an Exhibition, tiptoeing into the under-sized model of an ideal home. This was the miniature London house in the grand manner, here was the under-sized circular staircase, the small family portrait, marble topped hall table and baby chandelier. It was all none of his doing. He climbed the stairs.

Upstairs he searched the boxes in vain for a cigarette; silver and varnished wood, they gave him a faint smell of cedar and some grains of tobacco. Finally he found a crumpled packet in his dressing gown pocket. He lit his cigarette in the bathroom, his hand was shaking slightly, as if the lack of sleep had made him drunk. Daylight was coming into the house as it was meant to, gently infiltrating between yellow curtains like a well trained parlour maid with the tea. Kennet drew himself a cold bath, to satisfy, in this well-mannered house, a wild longing for discomfort.

He bathed, rubbed himself down and dressed again in fresh clothes. He went back into his bedroom and lit another cigarette. It was time for him, reluctantly, to take stock of the situation.

For a man who lived his life by a simple set of rules, loyalty to his family, to his clients, to his profession it was, he thought, as nasty a situation as he could wish to meet.

He had received a visit, the day before, from Vernon Hume, Mrs Monument's younger nephew. He had been outraged, blustering and sly. The object of his visit, Kennet had no trouble in deciding, was to discover the terms of his aunt's will for the purpose of raising money on his expectations. It had been easy for Kennet to adopt an attitude of offended propriety and put off his inquiries on the grounds that his instructions from Mrs Monument were confidential. But at the end of the interview Vernon Hume, pink faced and puffing like an outraged spinster, had said the words which had kept Kennet awake all night.

'You can put me off now but this is not the end of it. The whole family's on to what you and your son have been doing with Aunt's money. We're not putting up with it much longer.'

What Kit had been doing . . . When his work had finished that day he had started to go through the Monument papers. It was a complicated situation, with settlements which had their heads in the beginning of the last century and their culmination in the death of Gerry Monument. He checked the investments and assessed, as far as he could, Mrs Monument's private unsettled fortune. He lit cigarettes and beat like a dog among the bank accounts, profit and loss accounts and market figures. He tried to explain the conversion into cash of a woolshop in Birmingham, an ironmonger's in Luton and a hotel in Bexhill-on-Sea. He suspected the laconic plausibility of the income tax returns, the balancing of the business accounts. He worked feverishly, as if anxious to prove what he most feared. When he had worked it out once he did it again. The tenth demonstration proved nothing.

Nothing, of course, could have been proved. But there were things . . . The transfer of shares Mrs Monument had sent him to sign as a co-trustee, amounts shifted from safe concerns to more curious ventures. Large withdrawals, advances of cash which she had asked him to arrange and which he had not questioned. Looking at her letters again and again, comparing them with her earliest, meandering, contradictory communications, he began to doubt if Mrs Monument was responsible for the entire correspondence. There seemed to be a scheme behind what she was doing now, an astute and dangerous financial plan working out through her spidery handwriting, protruding among the underlinings, family chatter, and frequent exclamation marks of which her letters were composed.

But that it was Kit . . . Did Kit go down to Worsfold? Who were his friends besides the intolerable Porcher and the eccentric Mrs Monument? What, if anything, was the connection between them?

He saw himself suddenly in his dressing room mirror, the face frowned out at him, alert and mobile. He looked down from the mirror to his big, awkward possessions, stamped with his initials, the leather collar box, the yellowing ivory brushes, the great comb which had missed two teeth since his undergraduate days. Who are we, he thought, my son and I, and what are we after?

He realized he knew nothing about Kit, he had no materials, as far as Kit was concerned, for understanding the situation. The thirty years between them had been enough, it seemed, to slice a life in half, so that his son was a mystery to him.

He thought, before I do anything, anything at all, I must

find Kit. I must find out what he's after – I must talk to him.

He decided that and felt better. His chief feeling during the night, he realized now it was over, had been loneliness. He went down to the kitchen to fetch the tea. He wanted to talk to someone.

The kitchen was an ideal home again, its decoration was modern. His wife's rule had been Regency for the upstairs, functional for the servant. Among the plastic curtains, birchwood furniture and built-in cupboards the Austrian girl stood rubbing the sleep out of her eyes and looking faintly dirty. The kettle was boiling over. As Kennet came in she jumped, as if he had been a firework that had suddenly gone off behind her.

'That's all right, Sophy. I'll take the tea up when it's ready.'

He sat down on a functional stool, designed to fit under the kitchen table, It was as comfortable as a small, neatly pointed tombstone.

'No need for waiting, Mr Kennet. That's ready.'

He embarrassed her, he thought, as she embarrassed him. The small bright eyes, looking out of a puffy face, what starvations, rapes, shootings, sudden arrests had they seen? He felt apologetic for his smoothly run house, where a stain on a tablecloth was greeted as a major disaster. He looked up at the wireless set his wife had bought her, printed under it was a neat list of the times she was allowed to play the thing. Sophy, he was inclined to say, what in hell are we doing in this galley? Let's go out and pawn the spoons and buy ourselves a ticket to some place where the sun shines all day and cockroaches infest the kitchen and there's a decent chance of winning a state lottery. Instead he said:

'Thank you. I'll take it up now.'

Quietly, unsmiling, he pushed open his wife's bedroom door. He put the tray down very carefully on the painted bedside table, afraid its clatter would waken her. He didn't draw the curtains. She was sleeping hungrily, anxious to drag every drop of refreshment out of her swoon. She slept like someone pulling the last puff out of a cigarette, her eyebrows drawn together, her mouth pursed. Her hair was cramped down under a net and Kennet knew that if she was awake she would have minded him seeing her so. He sat down on the bed beside her: her body made only a small ridge under the bedclothes. Five minutes ago he had itched to be away from the whole business, from the interior decoration, the trivial comforts, the tense, unhappy politeness of their daily conversation. Now he felt a sense of calm, almost a tenderness which his wife evoked as she lay unconscious, in a position in which she wouldn't have liked to have been overlooked.

In five minutes he knew, she would have to waken, face the endless, meticulous performance of her day, restore, with her make-up, her unchangingly smooth, hard, unreal attitude to himself. He would have liked to have saved her the trouble. He felt for a pipe in his pocket and lit it carefully, throwing the dead match at a Georgian fire bucket and effortlessly missing. He would have liked to have saved them both the trouble of starting this awful day, the day when they would neither of them get drunk or hit each other or run away with the servant, but would carry on, soberly, hopelessly and without enthusiasm with running the house, being married to each other and trying to disentangle the business affairs of Mrs Hester Hume-Monument.

At his wife's bedside stood her water carafe, her biscuits and a pile of books in smart coloured wrappers with modern typography that went with the curtains. He lifted one, a book of poems and read at random:

> *For all the nightmares I am worthy of,*
> *I wrap and post to my brown paper love.*

For a while he sat staring at the page, resentfully, like someone who, having been lost a long while in a strange countryside, at last finds a sign post which has been written in a moment of puckish humour by an imbecile. Then he thought that whatever it was and whatever they meant the lines just about summed it up.

'Christopher. What *are* you doing?'

'Eh? Oh, I'm sorry, darling. Here's your tea.'

'Yes, I can see it is.' His wife was sitting up, tearing the net off her hair. 'Christopher, you don't have to smoke that pipe in here, do you?'

'Pipe? No, of course not.'

He went over to the fire bucket and shot some glowing tobacco at it. Quite a lot went on the carpet. He had his back to his wife, knowing that she was hurriedly repairing her face, careful not to turn round until she had finished.

'Where did you get to after dinner?'

'After dinner? I went back to the office.'

'Whatever for?'

He blew through his empty pipe. It was hot and smelt of chemical manure.

'A lot of work's been piling up. Nothing special.'

He turned round. She was sitting up in bed now, ready to be kissed on the forehead. He kissed her clumsily, almost missing her as he had the fire bucket. He said:

'Do you see much of Kit now? Talk to him, I mean?'

'Of course I don't. Ever since he went to that awful room. Can you imagine, a naked electric light bulb, and round the top of the wallpaper – a sort of frieze. As a matter of fact it mightn't be too bad a house only that slut of a woman just sinks down to the basement like a troglodyte . . . Her husband's no better. I bought Kit one of the big new white table lamps from Peter Jones.'

'Did we pay?'

'Why?'

'I should have thought Kit might have afforded it.'

This was the moment, he knew, to have exchanged confidences. He should have sat down on the bed again, refilled his pipe and told her all about it. She would have listened, her eyes turned up, smiling thoughtfully, her hands spread out on the counterpane, as she had in the first year of their marriage. I'm a bit scared, he could have said, scared and sick to the stomach from being up all night, and getting too old for this sort of thing. I can hear distant sounds like the start of an avalanche or the first shots in the native quarter of a revolutionary city and the hell with it. I want no part of it. I want to be left in peace.

'Poor boy. One has to do something for him. So I got them to box it up and just took it round in a taxi one afternoon when he was out. Well, I got this Urquhart to help me fix it up. First of all he had no screwdriver. I had to go out to Woolworth's and buy him one, and then, then there was the smallest blue flash – the man screamed so he might have been bitten by a snake . . .'

Among other things, he might have told her, you should know what Kit's up to. Not that I know, even after sitting up all night and smoking too many cigarettes so that my mouth tastes like the Leicester Square tube station and my eyelids feel like lead. But I can guess. My guess is he's trying to do something sensational with the rightful property of a valued client of mine who is so up to her eyes in gin that she can't tell what time of the day it is, with the result that there are going to be a lot of very angry relatives and a lot of very hungry horses in a village called Worsfold. They're not such nice people but they're our sort of people, trying to live our sort of life with a certain amount of honesty, and difficulty and courage. But Kit, Kit it seems, is a different sort altogether, we ought to find out why, we ought to find out what.

His wife lifted her cup to her lips, grimaced.

'Appalling tea. When shall we have an English maid again?'

'Is it? I thought it was rather nice.'

'Oh you. The trouble is, Christopher, you've got no standards. And you know I hate that tie.'

She put her cup down and lit her first cigarette.

The room was cold, the orange flame of her lighter was the only warm thing in it.

He said, 'I must go down and get some breakfast, I've got a lot to do today.'

'All right. Try and be out for lunch. I'm going to a sale.'

As he went downstairs Kennet remembered a poem he had once learned at school. He thought it was a much better poem than the one he had read at his wife's bedside. People, the poem had said, were like islands, when they tried to communicate with each other they noticed that, between them, there was a lot of very cold salt sea.

So she was going to a sale. By nightfall he would probably own another object, it might be a papier mâché tray, or a Victorian paperweight, or a set of sporting prints: the odds were it wouldn't be anything he was going to fall in love with.

3

Mad in Pursuit

The girl Anna woke early in Seton's flat and went into the kitchen to make tea. Domesticated movements, the gestures of everyday life, were obviously strange to her. For a while she stood bewildered before a great rusty gas cooker, a fitting which looked as if it might have been bought second hand from a troopship. Then she gingerly turned on a tap and, with the gas hissing, started to search for a match. With her lips pursed she explored the cups and pots on the dresser. After a search she found a trouser button, three pennies and a curious little enamel badge.

Seton had woken up in the sitting room next door and was standing, dressed in a long, dirty dressing gown, his sparse curls floating about his head, doing some breathing exercises he had read about in a book on Indian philosophy. Robed and sexless, he looked like an apoplectic monk or an aged contralto singer about to burst into song.

As he breathed he noticed that the comparatively pure air of Fitzroy Square was, to a great extent, mixed with gas.

He strode in a masterful way into his kitchen, threw himself at the cooker and turned off the tap.

'Don't do it, Anna!' he gasped. 'Don't do it, I beseech you!'

She looked at him puzzled but uninterested from the other end of the kitchen.

'I've always thought you were very "us", Anna. Tragic child of our time, that's what I called Maggie Upton when I talked about her on the wireless. Of course she wasn't

38

really a child, more like forty. But you're so obscenely young –'

'Who was forty? Who are you talking about? Have you got a match?'

Automatically, he gave her one from his dressing gown pocket. She turned on the gas again, lit it and started to boil the kettle.

'Maggie Upton, poetess and lover, morte au Charlotte Street, November 10th, 1945,' Seton was intoning, enjoying the sound of his own voice. He looked at the girl, feeling anxious and lonely, bitter yet excited. She was so young, so penniless, so proud, so utterly uninterested in that resounding pageant, the life, death, hopes and despairs of the poet Seton. His voice became more exaggerated as he went on. 'Isn't it in all of us somewhere? Karl Craxton, professor and pederast, drowned himself in the Cherwell, 1942. I've known it all myself. My suicide hours are nine to eleven, the worst months are January and February, after the nut harvest and before the stone fruit. Suicide places are London, Worthing and the suburbs of Paris. Darling little Anna, you'd be amazed how often I've sat in my bath like a great, grounded porpoise and thought of making a Roman end of it all with a safety razor blade . . .'

She was pouring hot water into the teapot now. Without turning round she said. 'Oh, shut up.'

It had always been the same, Seton reflected. The antics of poets never impressed those whom poets loved. London was no doubt strewn with girls, spectacled, enlightened, obese, who would have been fascinated by the reflections of Seton on the suicides he had known. Only this one, frozen into her youthfulness, forgot to listen. He was reminded of his school-days when, fat and inky, he had straggled to school behind the neat, hard Scottish children, the girls with fair plaits and tartan ties. Desperately, he had shouted obscenities, danced, fallen into puddles to attract their attention, and they had stared back at him, unamused. He hitched himself up on the edge of the table and put a hand on Anna's shoulder. If he could not impress the children he could help them with their homework, take the blame for the windows they had broken, arrange their love affairs.

'Don't worry,' he said. 'We'll find Kit today. Whatever he's doing, we'll find him.'

In a town so lived over as London, every street speaks with an accent, almost every house has a language of its own. The hieroglyphics are as many and involved as the Chinese alphabet, incomprehensible to foreigners, capable of infinite subtle variations of meaning to Londoners themselves. In point of distance it was not far from Kennet's house to Godiva Crescent, but the house he stood before when he got there was as different from his own as a skyscraper from St James's Palace or an igloo from a kraal. His own house was older yet more modern, cool, self-assured, in the fashion. 9 Godiva Crescent was a great ugly upright structure, approached by a flight of stone stairs to a doorway that seemed copied from the west entrance of Salisbury Cathedral by a jobbing builder with a squint. Below the front steps were inky areas of basement, freezingly dark kitchens, and large intractable boilers. It was difficult to imagine that anyone had ever had the grim self-confidence to live in the whole house. Now there were no less than eight separate bells, above each a square of cardboard, typed, printed or scrawled in violet ink, announced the names of the inhabitants.

Standing on the top step Kennet first tried the bell over which his own name was typed. Nothing happened so he rang the others, working from the bottom to the top. Then he worked from the top to the bottom. Peering through a window into what must have once been a dining room, a room designed for Turkey carpets, mahogany sideboards and paintings of dead birds, he saw within the gestures of a sparse modernity. There was a divan bed with a bright cover, a row of paper covered books, a lamp with a long chromium plated arm. He withdrew his head as suddenly there seemed to him to be someone in the bed.

At last the door was opened by an Indian in a long purple muffler carrying a pile of books. The Indian grinned at Kennet and went off on a bicycle, leaving the door open. Kennet went in gingerly, avoiding a pram. From the basement he heard the sound of a baby crying and he slowly, experimentally, went downstairs.

The baby was sitting forward on Sylvia Urquhart's lap. It had finished feeding and she was thumping its back with a big, flat hand, hitting it so hard you expected the small baby to fly up against the wall like a ping-pong ball after a heavy service. Instead it grinned and produced a faint belch, stretching out its nose toward Kennet like a mole stretching for the light.

Kennet stood in the doorway, cautious and apologetic, a big man in dark clothes and a bowler hat. Sylvia Urquhart had turned her head away from the baby to draw on a cigarette, her dressing gown was stained with milk and smeared with ash, and she didn't seem to have anything on underneath it. At the same time her hair was clean and soft, as if she washed it every afternoon because she hadn't anything else to do. Kennet thought she and the child looked remarkably healthy. He coughed and she looked round at him sleepily, without surprise.

'I'm sorry . . .'

'That's all right.' She went on patting the child automatically, its sausage arms were stretched out, its hands opening and shutting like the gills of a fish. Her dressing gown was open, scarcely covering her breasts. She peered at him inquiringly and then, as if she had only just appreciated his sex, put her hand to her throat and pulled the dressing gown to. 'Is it . . .' she screwed up her eyes, none of her friends had bowler hats, they were worn, in her experience, by gas inspectors, plain clothes policemen, possibly, although she had never seen one, by bailiffs. Yet Kennet was too healthy for a gas inspector and too well dressed for a detective. She couldn't rid herself of the idea, however, that his intrusion was due to Urquhart not having paid something he should.

'I was looking for my son. Kennet. I believe he lives here.'

It was nothing to do with them. Sylvia was relieved.

'Yes he does. He did. He's gone.'

'Oh, I'm sorry. Then I won't bother you.'

'No please.' She felt suddenly guilty, as if, not having produced this man's son she must offer him a worthy substitute, lunch, cigarettes, a bed for the night, even a cup of tea. 'Sit down a moment. I must just put the baby back.'

She disappeared.

Kennet didn't sit, feeling unwilling, somehow, to presume on so casual an acquaintance. He crossed over to the mantelpiece which was littered with objects, an evening paper, three days old, a card of safety pins, a post card reproduction of a painting by Braque, a china Highlander without a foot and a battered green tin alarm clock which, for no reason, chose that moment to ring raucously. Kennet stopped it affectionately, it was a clock such as his wife wouldn't even have allowed in a servant's bedroom.

He saw Sylvia in a spotted mirror over the mantelpiece. She was dressed now, in a white shirt and a pair of dark trousers.

She said, 'You've stopped it.'

'Yes I have. Is it for anything?'

'Only my husband. It's time for him to stop reading the paper and start writing his novel.'

'Really? Where is he?'

For an answer she pointed at the ceiling. Kennet looked respectfully upward, in silence they paid their tribute to the mysteries of creation. When Kennet spoke again, he did so softly, as if in church.

'That's a nice-looking baby you have.'

And then the room span, he put out his hand to grab the mantelpiece and missed it. To the girl's horror the great, solid man tottered, like an ancient building that has been picked at, night and day, by a demolition squad.

She held out her arms to save him, but he recovered and blinked, ashamed.

'Sit down. Is anything the matter?'

'No. Nothing. It's stupid.'

He sat down, too big for the spindly steel chair.

'I've been up all night. Too old for it. Tell me, do you know my son well?'

'Hardly at all.'

'Is that so? Neither, as a matter of fact, do I. By the way, what time does that clock of yours go off?'

'Ten o'clock.'

Ten o'clock. It was the time that, for the last thirty years, he had walked into his office, said good morning to his managing clerk, started opening his letters. He enjoyed the thought, as if he were on holiday.

For the moment they were silent. Sylvia Urquhart looked at Kennet. She's looking at me, he thought, as if I were an animal at the Zoo, an elderly patient animal or some dignified, musty species. She found a cigarette in a paper packet, turned it thoughtfully between her lips before she lit it, staring all the time. She's like a modern, wide-eyed child on the other side of the bars, aloofly licking a sweet. Not for the first time in his life, Kennet was filled with a wild desire to communicate, to say everything, to confess. It was a desire all his training and years had repressed so that now he was well able to speak to his wife, his clients, his friends at his club, without saying anything at all, without giving anything away, without losing face by betraying, in any unguarded moment, his loneliness, his unhappiness or his uncertainty. They had mentioned Kit, the opening was there – he could have spoken out to the woman in front of him – but what was the use? It would have sounded to her like the distant, surly bellow of the displaced bull in his cage, powerless and a little comic. She

43

couldn't help him; it was best to keep those matters to oneself.

So Kennet said nothing more about his son. There remained, however, the instinct of the bull to collect the women of the herd. He stood up, almost defiantly to show there was nothing wrong with him, and produced a silver match case from his waistcoat pocket. He felt the exhilaration of those about to embark on something that is both undignified and unwise.

'Won't you have a light?'

Sylvia Urquhart still stared inquisitively, then she leant forward to the flame between his fingers, which was burning as steadily as could be expected.

Above them Urquhart's hand was poised over the blank paper. His stomach felt as empty as his head. 'Christ,' he was saying to himself. 'And will it never be time for lunch?'

Mrs Kennet made an entrance down the staircase into the empty hall. No one saw her.

Cleaned, bathed and powdered, her still attractive and useful body was cunningly supported and compressed, clothed in a dignified black suit with a shirt that hid the loose skin about her neck. One hand, dangling jewellery from the wrist, patted the back of her head, the other held her exaggerated spectacles and a novel. She was frowning slightly, as if out of temper that all the washing and powdering, the nice choice of lipstick and the exact setting of a diamond clasp in her lapel should be wasted on the neat empty house, the carefully planned but vacant day ahead.

As a matter of fact she couldn't see very much without her glasses, which she carried in her hand from a lonely and self-sufficient sense of vanity. The hall, therefore, seemed blurred and dark to her, when the telephone started to ring.

For a while she regarded the white instrument on the marble topped, quilt legged, Empire hall table with revulsion. She enjoyed the telephone, lying in bed she could talk for half an hour at a time to the women she knew, her polite, effusive, deadly enemies. She often used the telephone with effect to destroy a grocer or annihilate a dressmaker, being, in that respect, unlike her husband who only acquired belligerency with a fountain pen. Now, however, the telephone upset her, attacking her off her guard in the hall when she was on the way downstairs to endlessly complicate the morning of Sophy, whom she could no longer bear to think of sitting in a comfortable lethargy, dipping a doughnut into a cup of over sweet coffee and tearfully recalling the shops in the Kärntnerstrasse. Moreover the telephone had a threatening and predatory tone, breathing disaster.

The uncomfortable quality of this telephone call was exaggerated by the fact that Mrs Kennet was kept in suspense long after she had lifted the receiver. The voice, apparently, was seeking to speak from some remote part of England, and had to be assisted from provincial town to provincial town to the accompaniment of clicks and buzzes and the wearied instructions of rustic operators. Finally the lines were cleared and the female voice rushed at her untrammelled. The words came galloping out in a voice desperate and almost out of control, a voice like a horsewoman embarking on a hideous fence, the only possible outcome of which will be a broken collar bone and calls for a hurdle. To Mrs Kennet the voice also carried the picture of the icy hall in which the caller was speaking; there seemed to be a suppression, with difficulty, of the chattering teeth.

No, Mrs Kennet answered, her husband was not at home, he was at his office. Not at his office? That was curious but he must certainly be on his way. No, he would not be home until after six, he would have lunch possibly in the City, probably at his club – then if she would care to telephone the hall porter? Should she take a name – Mrs Peggy Monument? Yes, she'd tell her husband . . .

'I'll take it.'

An arm in a dark overcoat encircled her from behind and took the receiver carefully from her hand.

'Yes. Kennet speaking. Oh, she has, has she? No. There's

nothing for her to worry about. Tell her we'll hold them a little longer, a week maybe, then we'll sell. Tell her I'll be down. Yes. I'll come down at once. I'll explain it all to her.' He laughed, 'No. I can get down by myself, thank you.'

Mrs Kennet stumbled on a high heel, out from between the telephone and her son.

'Kit! I never heard you come in. How did you manage it?'

'I've got a key. How are you, Mother?'

He put the receiver down and turned round to look at her, his hands in his overcoat pockets.

'You've got a key? Then why don't you come here often, Kit? I'd have thought you'd have done anything to get out of that awful little room. You're staying, aren't you? I'll tell Sophy about lunch.'

The change had come over her in less than a minute. She had softened into a middle-aged anxious woman, peering up at her son with eyes that waited to be hurt.

'I'd like to – but I've got to go.'

'Just for lunch, Kit. I was going to a sale, why couldn't we go together? French furniture, we might get you something for your room. Wouldn't you like something really amusing for your room?'

'I don't want any furniture, you know. No furniture at all.'

'Kit, you're so curious. You seem to hate having things. Constance was reminding me the other day how, when you were just fifteen, she and Peter wanted to buy you a model aeroplane, with an engine, that really flew, and you said thank you you'd rather have the money. Can you remember?'

'No.' He put his hand on her shoulder, lightly, as if to calm her. 'I'm sorry, I'll come again some time.'

'Kit, your father's disappeared somewhere. He's not at his office apparently, he'll be out all day. It'll just be the two of us. Won't you stay?'

Kit Kennet frowned.

'Father? Where's he gone to?'

'How should I know? Some dreadful law court, I suppose. He tells me nothing. I don't know anything at all nowadays – where you're going, for instance?'

'A village in the Midlands. It's very cold and nearly everyone there owns a horse.'

'Cold? Kit, you will keep your overcoat on, won't you; where on earth will you find to stay? Send me an address when you get there. Horses do you say? Well they can't be altogether disreputable people, I should have thought. But Kit, can't you catch a train after lunch, I'll run down and tell Sophy?'

But the front door had opened and shut and she was left alone in the hall, her arm extended in a curiously theatrical gesture of longing and despair.

4

And in Possession So

As the train pulled out of Paddington, Kit looked at the bombed houses at the side of the railway line. They had all been smashed ten years ago, and ten years ago he had been a boy who hadn't noticed houses anyway. To his father, perhaps, the whole thing had come as a great surprise. When Kit looked at a house, or a city church, he almost expected to see it degutted and demolished, with the fireplaces stuck ridiculously on an outside wall.

It was a dirty, steamy first class carriage with dark blue seats. Opposite him sat an American flying officer and a girl in a white sweater. The American had a face like sauerkraut with gold rimmed spectacles, the girl looked at Kit and he stared thoughtlessly back, as if he had seen them both, like advertisements, a hundred times before.

He picked up his newspaper and began to read it backwards, first the market prices and then an account of a boxing match. He read at some length the story of a murder in a French provincial town. The front page was filled with news from the Middle East; he had read it earlier on.

After Reading the American put his arm round the girl's shoulder and gave her a sheet of cleansing tissue on which she blew her nose. An old man in spats ostentatiously left the compartment. Kit worked out the probable result on Mrs Monument's foreign holdings of the day's news. In his mind figures and men were added and subtracted together. He made little distinction between them.

He thought, for instance, of Mr James Porcher and the

hotel in Margate where he had talked to him. A violin had mewed endlessly behind the palms, the hotel air was heavy with pipe smoke and the delegates were somnolent after three days' over-eating, listening to speeches and obedient voting. In dark suits, with cryptic brass badges in their button holes, they lay in arm chairs, uncomfortable and distended. In a group beneath the most exotic palms, perched on the edge of their chairs as if a diversity of internal complaints prevented relaxation, their wives chatted and knitted. Plain, past middle age, these women clung together in alarm, feeling that they had lost the interest of their husbands, had failed to understand the speeches, and seeing in their futures as the wives of government officials nothing particularly to look forward to.

Porcher had taken Kit out past his own wife without speaking a word to her. Their love was something he had finished with long ago, like pacifism and the Independent Labour Party, and which he knew could not possibly help him now.

Kit remembered the dark Promenade, the distant complaint of the sea, the lamps shining on the girls who walked home arm in arm munching fish and chips and humming popular songs. He remembered that Porcher had agreed to the deal he suggested, not for the money involved, but because he wanted to show that he had the power to do it. It was an act done in the darkness to impress a silent, unimpressionable man of half his age, an act of quite pointless exhibitionism. It was as if he were saying, I am Porcher, I am in now and I can make things happen, anything I like. These, of course, were not his words, and what he had said was, 'I used to come here as a lad. No Excelsior Hotel for Ivy and me then. A sit on the beach and a packet of fish and chips and then the bike back to London, me talking all the day about reforming the world most likely. Things have changed a bit since then . . .'

But Kit knew that when Katz was ready to dispose of the stuff, it would be ready too. Katz was an operator with a glass eye which he had got at Anzio, and now lived by manufacturing something in a converted garage in Paddington and did all right for himself. Kit thought he understood Katz. He would rather have been with Katz than this man on the promenade who had gone on to stare with some hunger at a pair of girls who had been walking in front of them. This Porcher who fooled Porcher all of the time, this old Porcher who had run out on the young Porcher and would, no doubt, in time run out on everyone else. Kit smiled to himself. Before that happened he would have run out on Porcher.

As the countryside, grey, wet, uninviting, streamed by, Kit lay back and closed his eyes. His thoughts, simple, hard calculations of ways to make money, were, perhaps, his only genuine concern. It was possible, however, that they were the gestures of a rôle he had built up for himself, part of a character that he had desired and now believed himself to be. Although he sat motionless, he was still nervous and excited, as if the plan he had worked out were his first love affair. In fact he was in love with the world he had found, the discovery of which he had made by himself and quite alone.

'You'll have to find out for yourself, Kit,' his father had said, a long time back, the last time when they had had any conversation of importance; conversations of importance with his family were things from which his father instinctively withdrew himself, like scenes in front of the servants. 'What you think is right, what you think is wrong, what you find detestable and what makes you happy – you'll have to find it all out for yourself. No one else can tell you.' There was another saying of his father's which Kit remembered: 'If preachers talk to you about the purpose of life, remember its purpose is being alive. Being alive's enough.' At the time, he recalled, he had doubted if that were true. He had found it difficult, indeed, to understand what great satisfaction his father drew from life, carrying on the respectable business of a family lawyer, lunching at his club, visiting the picture galleries by himself on Saturday mornings to stand, for half an hour at a time, before a sketch by Renoir or Degas.

During their talk, which had happened while Kit was still at school, he had felt that there was more to the preachers than his father allowed. Just too young for the war, he had done his military service when it was over, and learnt to fly. In flying he had felt his deepest emotions but, generalized conversations between them having long ceased, he had not confided those emotions to his father. He had come back from the Air Force with a longing for the war which he had missed, an inability to find satisfaction in the love affairs which presented themselves, and a deep contempt for the well-intentioned Welfare State which Mr James Porcher helped to direct.

Estranged, by a shyness that early beset them when alone with each other, from his father, Kit had transferred his admiration to the older men who had taught him flying, the shocked remnants of the bomber crews and fighter squadrons who nervously avoided the return to civilian life, men who lived on gin and cigarettes and became calm and reassuring only in the air. They had known about dogs and second-hand cars and he had joined in their parties. At one of these parties he had met Katz, a remnant of the Army who had gone back to civilian life as if it were a Commando raid. Talking to him, Kit had first learned to feel about money as if it were a dangerous occupation, as if a stuffed note-case were a symbol of virility like a bayonet.

He had remembered Katz when he had gone back to work for a while with Kennet's firm. There he had immediately discovered the side of people for which his father made no allowance, their price and their passionate self-interest. Quietly, contemptuously, Kit had been in the know. He had a knack of getting people to confide in him, not because they liked him but because they wanted to impress him. Oddly his timeless youthfulness made them want to please him, and Kit became a successful operator among dealers on the stock market, speculative business men and the hangers-on of politics. He dealt with these people aloofly, silently, as if he were taking a revenge on life for those men whom he had admired and who had been unable to return to it.

He had left his father's firm before completing his articles. He was on his own, as he liked to say, living by himself in a room he rented because his mother's presence gave him a feeling of suffocation, like having too many blankets on the bed in summer, and because he had no interest in living with a woman.

The Hume-Monuments had been friends of his family and among the first of his father's clients with whom he had made contact. He and Gerry Monument had been at school together for a short while, and later Mrs Hume-Monument's backing had helped him in the various concerns in which he was interested. So far they had been successful, but before his latest deal became possible his speculations had almost grown too easy. His business with Porcher had, however, the fascination of a night attack, daring, rewarding if it succeeded, fatal if it failed.

It was Katz who had first told him about the possibility of buying surplus weapons from the Ministry, weapons that had been scheduled for destruction. Katz who opened a bottle of whisky for him in his office in Paddington and told him about the deal and the profit to be made by anyone with a bit of capital and a client to receive the stuff. It only needed working on by someone with contacts. Kit had said he had known where he could raise the capital.

There had followed months of preparation, interviews with puffy, frightened men in blue suits who seemed to stare at Katz like rabbits at a snake, visits to dumps in the country, the careful tapping of clients who might be interested. Rumours of an inquiry, sudden dismissals, had held up the business for months: but the trail had led quietly and certainly to Porcher in his seaside hotel.

It was a long time now since Katz and he had first talked

over the scheme. It had become essential to them both, it had to come off. When Kit had spoken of the possibility of someone talking, of rumours leaking out and leading to a prosecution, Katz had said, 'No one's going to talk,' and, as he opened his safe to put the bottle of whisky back, Kit had seen the butt of a revolver protruding from a tin tray.

That was why these difficulties with Mrs Monument had to be straightened out. She was the source of the capital they needed. The job would be over soon, there wasn't much longer to wait and then anyone could look at her accounts, Katz would celebrate at the White City and Porcher could go on holiday to Bournemouth. At the moment things were tricky.

So Kit opened his eyes as the train drew into the station, stabbed a cigarette at the corner of his mouth and lit it with a lighter that always worked first time. It would have been difficult to say if these were the gestures of a man of genuine competence, or of a nervous boy seeking reassurance which he had always needed and had never, so far in his short life, found.

'Just another little one, perhaps. Up to the pretties.'

'Not good for you. I want you to understand some business.'

'So dull. Have you seen how I've changed the room round – and admire my new monkey musician. Peggy went up to Town and bought him specially for me in the King's Road.'

On the mantelpiece a china ape in eighteenth-century costume grappled with a double bass.

'I don't like them,' Kit said. 'My mother collects them.' He got up and fiddled with the ornament. 'Must have cost a lot of bran mash though.' His eyes wandered up to the portrait. 'How's Gerry?'

'Gerry?' Her long, ringed fingers scrabbled in her work basket. 'I don't think I've had a letter, not this week.' She found an envelope with an Air Force crest. 'No, this is an old one.' Suddenly her voice became plaintive, like a disappointed child's. 'Kit, how could you ask me how he is when you know he's –'

'Dead. But he's still the liveliest character in this village.'

She smiled hazily through her tears. 'Perhaps that's right. The others haven't got Gerry's fire, have they?'

'Not so interesting, anyway.'

'Kit – I don't want you to be cross about this, but they've all been on to me. All the others, I mean. Rolley's got some idea about riding stables, and their school fees are all coming in at this time of year. I think I'd like to know just how I stand. I think I ought to get your father down and go into it thoroughly.'

Kit walked back across the room and sat down by the bed. She had spoken kindly and he was taken off his guard. For a moment he felt he would have liked to have thrown his hand in, a hand that, despite its promise for the future, at the moment contained not even a pair of twos and certainly no joker. Instead, he said, 'All right. We'll go into it all in the morning. Everything you've got's quite safe. You can't sell now, though, the market's not right.'

'Very well, Kit – the morning. But I warn you, they'll be round tonight. Like kites on a battlefield, as Gerry used to say. Did you know him very well?'

'Not very.' They had had this conversation a dozen times. 'I was at school with him, of course, but I was younger, only fourteen when he . . . left. Then we went out together once or twice during the war. I was still a schoolboy. Had some good evenings, though.'

One of the good evenings: in the bar of a deserted hotel off Piccadilly during the war. Kit and Gerry were looking at each other across an ash-strewn tablecloth. Gerry was in uniform, Kit in a blue suit rather too small for him. A lonely tart in a black satin dress leant over the bar and helped herself to a crème de menthe. Gerry was drinking brandy and talking in a high, cracking voice. 'It's the face, the things they can do to your face that gets you. I don't care where they hit you so long as they leave your bloody face alone.' The crashes outside shook the bottles on the bar. Later Kit took charge of Gerry's gold bracelet watch in case the tart stole it off him in bed.

'They talk about Gerry to please me down here,' Mrs Monument said, 'but I don't think they really liked him. He wasn't like the Humes any more than his father was. I think they thought them both a little common.'

Kit looked back at Gerry. Poor sap, with his too narrow moustache and his too close-set eyes and his too wavy hair. He hadn't been very nice or particularly honest, and his lechery had been both furtive and ill-concealed. During the short period of his adult life he had been, for most hours of the day, tight, pugnacious and scared silly. The clubs he tried to join blackballed him, the girls he went to bed with soon acquired a distaste for him, the cheques he wrote bounced higher than high heaven. Old men called him objectionable, shop girls called him lovely. In fact he was neither; but at least he hadn't lived on as though nothing had happened, he hadn't bought a tweed hat and married a girl with buck teeth and become an estate agent. He had been scared enough and reckless enough and unhappy enough to get himself mixed up in his day and age, and finally he had got himself blown up in an aeroplane and died in a way to which no one could take the slightest exception. 'Cheer up, Gerry,' Kit said to himself. 'You're all right.' And he drank from his glass, which Mrs Monument had filled with neat gin up to the pretties. Then he put his hand inside his coat.

'There are one or two things I want you to sign. Share transfers.'

'Not now, Kit. I tell you – they're all coming for drinks.'

'When you like, then. You're right that they never liked Gerry.'

He looked back at the portrait. You understand, he said, but not aloud, one's got to look after oneself first.

★

Downstairs, they were all waiting in the long living room which, while still the warmest living room in Worsfold, was, by reason of its infrequent use, still cold. There was the usual Worsfold open fireplace and the chimney down which you could drive a carriage and pair or a hundred mile an hour gale with equal rapidity. In the vast grate an electric fire burned behind some cellophane coal and papier mâché logs. Within freezing distance of the fire, dressed in tweed suits, cardigans, thick socks and sensible shoes, the Hume family were disposed on the chintz. Their expressions varied between the sullen, the puzzled and the determined. They had the appearance of English travellers abroad who have missed a vital train, sullen at their misfortune, puzzled at the duplicity of foreign taxi drivers and the unreliability of foreign time-tables, determined to raise the matter strongly with the British Consul at the earliest opportunity.

Prowling uneasily behind the sofas, munching cocktail biscuits whenever he got the chance, as if to add some vague benison to the occasion, was the Vicar of Worsfold. The presence of this hungry, haggard and practically faithless cleric subdued the gathering, prevented them from speaking their minds and increased the tension.

The family present were five in number. So firmly linked that they were two brothers married to two sisters and, the odd man out, Major Hume, Mrs Monument's brother. So far as the married couples went, nothing but their status in years seemed to have guided the brothers in their choice of a wife. Rolley, the eldest Hume nephew, had married Peggy, the elder Slingsby sister; the younger, Sandra, had naturally fallen to Vernon. Major Hume had never married. He was a short, spinsterish man, whose legs, in the big chintz chair, hardly touched the ground. His grey hair was closely cropped and his face was so rosy that it had a slightly unhealthy look, as if it had been rouged.

On the sofa, Rolley sprawled his legs straight out. He was biting his moustache and trying to clean his nails with the blunt end of a match. Beside him, his wife Peggy, the most determined of the lot, sat upright, her feet lost in the high, fur-lined boots which she was wisely never without. Her hands were clasped so that her knuckles showed white, her face was lined with the efforts of her life, the effort of keeping two unprepossessing boys at a minor public school, the effort of keeping the grocer quiet, the incessant effort of keeping Rolley out of the perpetual sulk which was his natural frame of mind. With one ear she was listening to her brother-in-law Vernon's monologue. With the other she was straining for the faintest sound from upstairs.

Sandra sat perched on the arm of her husband's chair. Only a slight failure of courage at some climax of her early life had, it seemed, prevented her from being pretty. It was as if, at a vital stage of her development, her breasts had lacked the confidence to fill out, her mouth to widen or her hair to wave and shine. As it was she was colourless, sharp featured, almost plain. She frowned, and pulled at the string of pearls round her neck. Puzzled, totally inexperienced as she was, facing the whole world like some hostile and foreign country, there was, for Sandra, some hope. There was just the chance that she might one day discover what an intolerable bore her husband was and sink, at last, into the happiness of a love affair. She had a pale complexion, shading to pink round the nose and ears, which some lonely man might, in the future, find pitifully attractive. At the moment, however, she sat obediently on the arm of her husband's chair and listened to him saying, as he had said at least once a day during the last five years, 'Am I going to stay? That's what I'm asking the country. Is the Government going out or am I going to Rhodesia? I've put the issue squarely to the country this time. Are they going to keep us – or is it Africa now?'

Sandra continued to pull nervously at her pearls, seeing the mangy, man-eating lion at the water hole, the witch doctors dancing in the dust and herself in a topee, lashed to a totem pole whilst the pots were heated.

Vernon Hume was nearly ten years older than his wife.

All his blood seemed to have rushed to his head, for he was of a scarlet complexion, he had brown curly hair and a small-featured, doll's face. His mouth was small and curved, like the mouth in a painting of an early Georgian whore.

'Give them another year,' Major Hume said, swinging his legs and talking with the clarity and vivacity of a rather superior ventriloquist's doll. 'Give them another year and they'll ruin the country.'

'Another year,' said Peggy Monument, 'and we'll all be ruined. Never mind the Government.'

Rolley sighed heavily and bit his moustache.

'Has Kennet come down yet? asked Vernon. 'Peggy, did you get hold of him?'

'I told you, Vernon, I rang up this morning.'

'We've got to get something definite out of him, have some check on what the old girl's doing.'

'Ssh!' Peggy indicated the vicar with a gesture of her eyebrow which, in happier days, had suspended a family quarrel in the presence of servants.

'Sorry, Vicar. Didn't notice you there. How's business?'

'Six in church only, yesterday.' The vicar blew out this lamentable figure with a cloud of biscuit crumbs. 'Not counting myself, naturally.'

Everyone was silent. Sandra looked round desperately, as if it had just got to her turn in a peculiarly difficult party game.

'We'd come, only there's no one to do the washing up on Sunday morning and Vernon likes such an enormous breakfast. How are the children, Peggy?'

'Flourishing. Dr Taylor says Jimmy may get into the third eleven if we can keep on another term.'

'We'll keep him,' Rolley mumbled from the sofa. 'Jim'll have his thirders. I'll see to that.'

'How's Nicholas, Sandra?'

Sandra wriggled on the arm of her chair. Nicholas was the best looking member of the family, a blond and rather soppy little boy of five who sometimes wore his hair in a slide.

'Lovely, of course.'

'I saw him on his pony today.' Rolley moved irritably as he spoke. 'Boy looked scared. Bit of a cissie, isn't he?'

Sandra blushed slowly from the neck upwards. Her two emotions, love of her son and hatred of her brother-in-law, were of surprising strength. Her loathing of Rolley had started on a summer day during their childhood when he had found her diary and shouted extracts from it to make the other children laugh. It had deepened during the first winter of her marriage when Rolley, drunk after a Hunt Ball, had tried contemptuously to make love to her. Even now the sight of his ugly, brick-red hands made her shudder, she tried not to look at the square, clumsy fingers with their patches of hair below the joints. She was still blushing when she said, 'He loves his pony. Of course he's not a cissie.'

Peggy smiled complacently; neither of her children could have been accused of any suspicion of physical beauty.

'Nicholas'll be all right,' Vernon asserted, 'when we can send him to a good public school.'

'Like coals to Newcastle.' Kit had intruded on them silently, and now stood by Peggy offering her a cigarette. He met their appalled, hostile eyes with a look of cheerful indifference. He seemed in the best of tempers.

'Is your father upstairs?' Rolley spoke first.

'No. It was bad luck he couldn't get down. Tied up in London. There's nothing to worry about. I've been through the whole thing with Mrs Monument.'

'The devil you have!' Vernon rose from his seat, disregarding his wife's hand on his arm as well as the surprised, sheep-like gaze of the vicar. 'What authority have you got for prying into Aunt's business affairs? That's what we'd like to know!'

'Vernon, please . . .' Peggy sighed; another dreadful, useless masculine scene, such as when the pipes burst or the butcher forgot to deliver.

'No, Peggy. We've got to have this out some time. What authority has he?'

Kit said, 'None at all.'

'Ah.' Rolley frowned hard, unable to think of the right thing to say.

'Except the authority your Aunt gives me. When she says I may, I'll discuss her business affairs with you as well. Until then we'd better go on quietly drinking her gin and talking about the weather. Had any sunshine this year?'

'There was one bright Sunday, I seem to remember, during Lent.' The vicar spoke suddenly out of the silence, like one inspired to utter at a Quaker meeting. 'It rained in the afternoon, of course.'

'We're not going to be put off, Kennet, you know. Sooner or later we'll have to talk about the whole thing.'

'Vernon, this is hardly a suitable time.' Major Hume beamed round in a soothing manner. 'We mustn't mix business with – ah, thank you, dear boy.' He took a drink from Kit with a flourish, as if he had just brought off a conjuring trick. 'Pleasure.'

'You've come from London?' Sandra had been watching Kit move round the room. As she spoke she coloured from the neck upwards.

'Yes. Do you ever go there?' Kit answered as if they were alone. She replied wth reckless terror, 'About once a year. To the dentist, for Nicholas.'

'Then we must meet.'

She looked silently back at him, as if she had started by trespassing in a private garden and then trodden on a snake. 'Vernon goes more often,' she whispered.

'I haven't been to London,' once more the vicar saved the situation, 'since my curate days. Tell me, is there still a Lyons Corner House?'

'Damn few jaunts to London for anyone,' Vernon almost shouted, 'unless we can get this money business sorted out. Where is Aunt, anyway?'

'Here she is, Vernon – all present and correct!' sang Mrs

Monument, gliding into the room. With varying degrees of difficulty the men rose.

'Hullo, boys. How are you, Padre? Sit down, do. Just a small one, Kit darling. Up to the pretties.'

Mrs Monument had dressed for the occasion in a costume appropriate for a cocktail party in Knightsbridge. She wore a small, smart hat, although she had come straight from her bedroom. She had on a black dress, not completely done up at the back, and a row of pearls. Her black suede shoes were stained about the heels with Worsfold mud. Above them, her thin legs in nylon stockings looked thin and white as matchsticks. She sat in the largest arm chair holding her gin and grinning at her brother.

'Bottoms up,' she said. 'Here's to the good old Duke.'

'Mrs Monument,' Kit said, 'the assembled family would like to talk about your money.'

There was silence. Vernon went a deeper red. Rolley bit harder on his moustache. Sandra whispered, 'Oh dear,' and stared at the tip of her shoe. The vicar studied the titles of the books in the bookshelf, Peggy took a deep breath and Major Hume carefully blew his nose on a yellow silk handkerchief.

Mrs Monument looked round innocently. 'Money? Surely not? Never talk about money at a party, Gerry used to say. Such a shame Gerry isn't here. He'd have played the gramophone. Can you play the gramophone, Kit?'

'I should think so.'

He took a set of 'Books of the Month' supported by china elephants off the radiogram. He switched it on and saw the last record Gerry had brought home still on the turntable. The Monuments arranged themselves to listen like a reluctant audience at a symphony concert.

> *Telling my arms that they will not miss you.*
> *Telling them lies*
> *As I doorstep kiss you . . .*

sang the record. It was the tune Gerry had heard at tea-time in a drinking club off Leicester Square, danced to in a night club in Uxbridge, the tune the R.A.F. band had been playing the night he took the W.A.A.F. out of the dance hall. It was the tune that the girl with shoulder-length hair and a big red mouth had whistled as she draped her stockings round the mirror of their hotel bedroom in Aberdeen, it was the tune he had played during his last week-end with his mother.

'Gerry danced to this,' Mrs Monument said. 'I once danced with him here. He said I was a wizard dancer. Nonsense, of course.'

Sandra looked at her in horror, afraid that the whole party might suddenly break into a macabre fox-trot.

Kit watched them, smoking but not drinking. In spite of himself, Vernon's foot began to beat time to the music. Peggy looked steadfastly in front of her. The vicar seemed out-witted, as if he had strayed, in all good faith, into a house where the Black Mass was regularly celebrated. The radiogram stopped with a sudden click, there were no more records on the machine. Mrs Monument blinked.

'Have another drinky, everyone. I must just go and give one to Cook. It keeps her in such a lovely temper.'

Unsteadily, but with dignity, Mrs Hume-Monument left the room.

'One of these days,' said Rolley, when she had left, 'she'll find out what sort that Gerry of hers really was.'

'She won't,' said Kit. 'And if you're wise you'll never try to tell her.'

After the family had left, the gramophone record was played again. And Mrs Monument and Kit Kennet danced to it.

Kennet put down the book he was reading and looked round the empty club library. He was doing, he knew, nothing that he ought to be doing. He had got no nearer to finding Kit or solving his problems. He should have been at home, where his wife was giving a cocktail party; his duty there was to smoke a pipe in the corner and occupy the duller guests. He was running away, escaping, taking refuge in this big, rather cold room, with its gilt-bound books and dark, barely recognizable paintings. If he had gone home, instead of coming here, he would not have done what had to be done; he would not have taken his wife in his arms and embraced her in front of an interior decorator, a Cambridge don, two successful broadcasters and the poet Seton, all of whom, at this moment, were drinking his gin; he would not have asked her why it was that after nearly thirty years of marriage they lived in such complete isolation from each other; he would not have found Kit and asked him why it was that in a generation tolerance should turn to ruthlessness, restraint to indifference, modesty to self-seeking. He would have failed in all that. He was probably better where he was.

He remembered his own father, a lawyer who had divided his life between making money and praying to God. Was he as incomprehensible to his own son, he wondered, as that remote, white-bearded ogre had been to him? Kennet was the product, not of his father, but of the schools and university to which he had gone. In his early twenties, at Kit's age, Kennet had discovered his creed. It had never altered and, although he still believed in it strongly, he still found it difficult to define. He had the faith of an early atheist in the conventions, the respectabilities of life. He would perform, like a Stoic, what he knew was expected of him; his behaviour was strictly regulated by his belief in the ultimate pointlessness of existence. From his University days he had known that he would take over his father's business, that he would marry a good-looking, irreproachable girl from a minor county family, that he would have a well-furnished London house and invite people to dinner. He had done all this with the meticulous care which an agnostic priest might devote to ceremonial or a Socialist Court official to matters of precedence. He had done it because he believed that without it his life would have fallen to pieces, drifted away, been spent. He lived, he would have told himself, because living as he did was an end in itself.

And yet beneath it all Kennet was, in terms of the last century, a man of passion. In the books he read, the pictures he admired, in his approach to life itself, he favoured the realistic, the masculine, the mundane. In the works of the Impressionist painters a naked shop girl is discovered, occasionally, next to a man in a top hat. Kennet could understand that man. The pleasures of the flesh were absorbing, necessary and great; it was still important to wear a high hat and, at some stage of the evening, bite on the end of a cigar, call a cab and return home.

In Kennet a type of middle-class Englishman had, in a sense, reached its culmination. The brutality and cunning which had brought the Kennets' original wealth had been refined and educated away. Cruelty had become unthinkable to him, dishonesty absurd, intolerance seemed to him the greatest sin. His feelings ran deep, yet any emotional display caused him profound embarrassment. He would never have said in so many words that he loved his son, although it was the truth. The characters of today, the puritan, the decadent, the deliberate neurotic, were incomprehensible to him. He understood, above all, the man of moderate sensuality who kept his head.

Being as he was, he had become a stranger, it seemed to him, to his own family, and his nature prevented any demonstration which might have cured the situation. He had no idea what Kit was doing or why he was doing it, and his wife had, long ago, frozen into an unapproachable life of her own. Deprived, by a failure in sensuality, of the normal, everyday compensations of womanhood, she had fallen back as she approached middle age on culture. In another age she would have become coldly religious, even entered a sisterhood. As it was she embraced the world of modern Art. In West End galleries, perfectly dressed, she and the smooth, abstract statuary could be seen regarding each other without emotion. In Mayfair cinemas she sat quietly watching those fashionable films which deal, modishly and incomprehensibly, with the subject of death. She bought surrealist pictures, intended to chill the already under-heated blood. In them the man with the naked girl wore, not a top hat, but a surgical mask and rubber gloves. She ate meals planned by American dieticians and slept with the aid of a battery of chemicals. The expensive clothes she wore were designed to attract no one, the comfort of her house gave none of her family any pleasure. Everything in her life seemed calculated to isolate her from the man she had married.

So Kennet sat alone in the club library, nursing the book on his lap and staring in front of him.

'Reading?'

Kennet looked up, seeing the lower folds of Porcher's waistcoat, the underneath of his chin, the bottom of his curly pipe which threw a halo of smoke round his smiling face.

'Oh – hullo. Not really.' Kennet shifted uneasily in his chair.

'What's the book?' The big hand descended remorselessly, seized the gilt volume and turned it over. 'Byron. *Don Juan.* Looks bad at your time of life, eh?'

'I'm afraid I've read it rather often, at all ages.'

Porcher squatted in the seat opposite, let out breath. Kennet felt persecuted, hemmed in.

'Seen the papers tonight? Fine thing, this Middle Eastern business. We'll handle them, though. No one's going to say this Government can't get tough when it wants to.'

'I haven't read the papers. I haven't followed the news out there just lately.'

Porcher looked at him, grinning. 'Don't keep track of politics much, I suppose?'

'Not much, nowadays, no.'

Porcher lay back in his chair and laughed, the volume of poems, which he still held, bouncing against his stomach.

'Not much? Dark horse, that's what you are, Kennet. Dark horse, you know.'

Porcher was still laughing when Kennet left the library. He didn't know what to do or where to go. He telephoned Godiva Crescent in the faint hope that Kit would have got back. Sylvia Urquhart answered the telephone and before he had stopped to think about it he found that she was accepting his invitation to dinner.

5
Sylvia

'So Kit's not here tonight?' The elderly young man in the stiff collar and drainpipe trousers bowed at Mrs Kennet over his glass.

'He's in the country.'

'Ah.' The young man breathed a sigh of relief. 'And your husband?'

Mrs Kennet shrugged her shoulders, bent her head over the orange flame of the match the young man offered her and blew smoke gently out of her pursed lips.

'Reading some Will, I always imagine him, to the assembled relatives – joining in port and biscuits and reading the Will.' Seton surged up to them, giggling and breaking in to the end of the conversation. He was excited and happy. Of all the sights calculated to stir his imagination, industrial landscapes, early railway engines, bones on a seashore, none stirred it more than the presence of well-to-do women. His toes wriggled appreciately as his feet sank into the carpet, his fingers caressed his glass of sherry, his eyes appraised Mrs Kennet's expensively tailored appearance.

The young man who, apart from being in the Foreign Office, wrote verse and appreciated Seton, tittered.

'Delightful,' he said. 'Delightfully nineteenth-century.'

'Tell me,' Seton asked Mrs Kennet, 'tell me, it interests me so, what does your Kit *do* in the country? He always strikes me as so urban.'

Mrs Kennet shrugged again. 'He goes away, I should imagine, because he wants to sort things out, to get away from it all and sort things out. He's running away, of course – the country means childhood, doesn't it? He'll come back.'

'Dear me!' Seton pulled a frightened face. 'How sinisterly maternal that sounds!'

Mrs Kennet turned abruptly away from him, not amused.

'But has he really gone?' the young man asked apprehensively. 'He's always so mysterious about himself, your son.'

'He's not mysterious. It's all quite simple and comes, no doubt, of having a nineteenth-century father. Seton, you can fetch me another drink.'

Seton rolled away obediently across the carpet.

Mrs Kennet said, 'When he gets home we must have a party for Kit. I'd like him to see more of you. You might ask him down to your cottage for the weekend. He ought to have some friends of his own generation.'

Terror came into the young man's eyes. 'The last time I saw him,' he muttered, 'when I suggested we might go to the Victoria and Albert one afternoon, he *was* rather hurtful about it.'

'Never mind. He's in a difficult position.' Mrs Kennet put her hand on the young man's arm. 'His father's got no idea what to do about him. You're so lucky to have escaped that father problem. I thought you might be a help to Kit.'

The young man breathed in heroically. 'I'll try, then, when he gets back. Now let me tell you *all* about Paris. You heard we saw Cocteau, of course?'

'So Tulkinghorn's not with us this evening?' Seton had returned with a small Martini and a large, rumpled looking publisher with horn-rimmed glasses who made this mysterious query.

'What do you mean?'

'Tulkinghorn, the enigmatic solicitor. That's what I call your worthy husband. I'd never read any titles by Dickens, but we're thinking of bringing out a Victorian Omnibus so

I read one – *Bleak House*. Great stuff. All about the mysterious Tulkinghorn. He gets killed.'

'Tulkinghorn.' The young man fizzed gently to himself as if he were the victim of some internal effervescence. 'What a wonderful name for him. From now on I shall always think of him as Tulkinghorn.'

'No, really!' Mrs Kennet smiled with half her mouth. 'No, really, I won't have him teased. Although he has surpassed himself lately. The other day he came home at about six o'clock in the morning – Sophy told me so.'

'Eccentric Tulkinghorn.' The publisher spoke without taking his cigarette out of his mouth, showering ash down his waistcoat. 'Perhaps there's a little woman in St John's Wood?'

They all laughed. 'Just a hard night among the deed boxes, wasn't it?' the young man asked.

'I think so.' Mrs Kennet stopped smiling. 'He's very conscientious. I believe he's a very thorough sort of lawyer, Apparently some tiresome old woman had got her affairs into a muddle . . .' She noticed the glazed looked that had come over her audience and stopped trying to explain. 'But it's really all too boring.'

The publisher said, 'I only pray he never takes it into his head to write a book about it all. You know, "Fifty years of a lawyer's life". Bound to be the most tremendous turkey.'

'Oh, he wouldn't do that.' Mrs Kennet gazed at some new arrivals as if hoping that by some miracle Kit might be among them. 'I can't even get him to write a letter. Dorothy, darling!' Bending at the waist Mrs Kennet moved towards her worst enemy, the young man's mother, a small, embittered woman with blue hair who was wearing, as a kind of gesture of contempt, evening dress. 'Dorothy, you look wonderful!'

'Mummy, but how splendid!' the young man joined in for an extra propitiation as he followed Mrs Kennet at a respectful distance.

'Well, I've got here,' the woman said, taking the handkerchief out of the young man's breast pocket and wiping a crumb off his chin. 'No thanks to that Bakerloo you told me about. And I suppose you're all about eight drinks ahead.'

'Talking of books,' the publisher said to Seton when they were left alone, 'when are you going to put pen to paper again?'

'Any time,' Seton said happily, 'when I've had some more of Tulkinghorn's gin. When I've had a great deal more of his gin.'

'It was a good idea, this, for me. I hardly ever have it.'

'Have what?'

'Dinner.'

'Good heavens, why don't you have it?'

'Well, I put the baby to bed. Somehow it takes a very long time. When I've done it, I feel awfully tired, and then Jim, that's my husband, has been writing all day, or trying to write, and he likes to go to the pub for a change at half-past six. So he's gone by the time the baby's stopped howling so – I don't know, I have a bit of bread and marmalade or something . . .' Sylvia gestured hopelessly. Kennet looked at her with intense curiosity.

'You must get,' he said, 'extraordinarily hungry.'

'So hungry.' Her hand pressed her stomach. She looked helplessly at the bill of fare. Incapable of choosing or deciding anything, the next few moments became, for her, a nightmare. When he took the enormous card out of her hands she was filled with gratitude.

'You probably don't like oysters, so we'll have smoked salmon, and the trout's all right, and a steak. The Alsatian wines aren't too bad for the fish. Can you drink claret?'

'Yes – yes, I think I can.'

She looked round the restaurant as if something in it might divulge the reason for her presence there. It was a small room with statues in glass cases and red wallpaper on which hung cartoons out of Vanity Fair, His Royal

Highness in the paddock at Epsom, Mrs Patrick Campbell, Dreyfus at his trial, and Mr Justice Darling. There were drawings by Phil May done on the backs of menus, signed photographs of Vesta Tilley and Queen Marie of Roumania. To Sylvia, they meant nothing, the spindly men with top hats and jutting cigars, the women with hourglass figures, but she rubbed her back against the plush and felt warm and comfortable.

They were almost alone in the restaurant. The aged waiter, after listening respectfully to Kennet, walked away with his knees slightly bent to mutter the order into a speaking tube.

Kennet looked at the woman beside him. He noticed the way she fitted her shoulders into the plush curve which was the back of their seat, her hair, the colour that had come into her cheeks, the way her throat grew out of the plain black neck of her dress. God alive, he said to himself, what do I think I'm doing?

'Was it all right,' he asked aloud, 'your coming out, I mean?'

'Oh, yes. After you telephoned I told the girl upstairs to listen for the baby, and Jim was out, as I say, so it was all right.' She was still puzzled, however, as to why she had suddenly plunged out into the night wearing her best dress and the only pair of stockings which weren't laddered, to eat this large and unlooked-for meal. Puzzled, but not worried.

'I'm sorry to be so unhelpful,' she said, 'about Kit.'

'Yes, Kit. Tell me, you know him – what do you think of Kit?'

'I don't know him, really. He's very attractive, isn't he?'

'Is he?' Kennet decided to give Kit a rest. 'Have some wine.' He fished the tall green bottle out of the bucket and enjoyed the way the coldness of the wine clouded the glass.

'Usually,' Sylvia said, 'I don't drink enough. I watch Jim drinking pints of beer and lend him back the housekeeping money all the time.'

Kennet said, 'It's good to drink, if you can get comfortable and no one rushes you.'

'It's not very comfortable in our pub. An awful draught under the door and they're always shouting "time" and turning the lights on and off. I like this, though.'

'It's lemonade, really. A sort of morning drink, like champagne. You want to drink it with breakfast in a strange town you've never been to before, or when you're waiting for a boat. Claret's different, you drink that in the evening when you feel quite safe and sure of yourself. I hope you'll feel like that when we come to it.'

'Oh, I do now.'

As a matter of fact she felt quite safe, a feeling mainly induced by the way in which he had ordered the food. Anyone else she knew would have asked her what she wanted, and a dreadful period of guilt and irresolution would have followed. She felt safe when told to take it or leave it, and when she took it she found it very good.

'What made you ask me here?'

Kennet said, 'I don't know. I was looking for Kit. I'd had some trouble at my office and a man called Porcher came and took away the book I was reading at my club. Besides, my wife was having a party.'

'I like parties.'

'You wouldn't like this one.'

'Why not?' She looked up at him from under the hair that fell across her forehead.

'Oh, because of the people. No, I suppose that's not fair. They might be worse. Very intelligent and all that sort of thing. Trouble is, I can never see their jokes. Tell me – Victorian chapels, do you find them funny?'

'No.'

'Neither do I. Just depressing. There's one fat fellow who comes, a sort of poet, he comes for the drink. He's not too bad. Of course you can't understand the stuff he writes, he doesn't expect you to.'

He frowned at the tall glass with its misty, gold, entwined initials and twisted it in his fingers.

Sylvia said, 'It annoys you, not understanding things.'

'I don't like it. I like to know where I am.'

'And you'd like to know where you are with Kit, isn't that it?'

Well, they might as well talk about it. He said, 'I suppose so. If he'd just been a great disappointment to me, as my father would have said, that would have been all right. I'd have liked it, and envied him a bit too, if he'd run off to live in Paris or got a girl in trouble or even taken to drink or gone into a monastery – well, I'd never have minded. Those are the sort of things I've longed, in a quiet way, to do myself. I suppose I should even have got some pleasure from buying annuities for his bastards, or keeping it all from his mother – you know the sort of thing, men rather enjoy it.'

'I should hate my son to go into a monastery. He could do the other things.'

Kennet looked at her. Her elbows were on the table and her chin was cupped in her hands; she was listening to him peacefully, like a tired child. The waiter brought the claret in a basket. Kennet tasted the wine cursorily and went on, 'But in what Kit does there seems to be no pleasure or happiness or belief. A certain amount of danger, perhaps, some power . . . I can't understand it. I never have been able to understand the desire to make a great deal of money. I suppose it's like wanting to fly too fast in an aeroplane or climb Mount Everest, uncomfortable sort of business it's always seemed to me.'

'I don't understand Kit, either,' Sylvia said. 'But then, I don't worry. I can't really understand my husband or what he's trying to write; and the lodgers, you know, do the most incomprehensible things.'

'It doesn't worry you?'

'Not a bit.'

He filled her glass. 'Do you like the wine? It's of the

year I bought for my club. It's smooth and strong and satisfactory and the only way of putting new blood into your veins when you get to my age. You can drink it at the heat of the room you're in, when the room's not too cold and the curtains are drawn and you're talking to a friend you've known for thirty years and discussing all the things you might have done with your life and what a good thing it is, on the whole, that you didn't do them. All the same, that's not the best way to drink it.'

'What's the best way?'

'In a restaurant, with a beautiful woman you're taking out for the first time.'

That, Sylvia thought to herself, is a compliment, a thing she had heard her mother speak of. She said, 'It's very nice. What a lot of nice things there are.'

They both laughed, and after that they watched each other, wary but content, wondering if, at any future time, they could trust their happiness to one another. The idea seemed safe and remote and it seemed to them both that if they did so, nothing terrible could go wrong. To Sylvia, Kennet appeared like her own father, a man who had never forgotten her birthday, who could lift her into the air on his arm, who had understood exactly what she had needed when he found her crying in the loft; the only man she had known who had never expected her to deal with his creditors or initiate lovemaking or get in the coal. And Kennet thought that with Sylvia he might know where he was, if she enjoyed things she would say so, and if not she would get out.

At ten o'clock they left the restaurant. The market at the end of the narrow street was empty; cabbage leaves and crumpled tissue paper lay in the gutters. A taxi nosed its way round the cobbled square, past the glass market build-ing, the barrows and piles of boxes. Sylvia saw Kennet signal the taxi. He took the cigar out of his mouth and she saw his big, greying head swathed in smoke under the street lamp, his eyes clear in the shadows and his chin stuck into the silk scarf round his neck. The rest of him, in his dark overcoat, seemed broad and solid as a house. Beside him she felt ridiculously light, as if, were it not for a great effort of will, she could have floated up into the sky. Then she was alone in the taxi, smelling the comforting smell of rexine, on her way home, trembling slightly as if she had just, on a hot summer day, dived into the sea.

6

Government Stock

The man Katz sat on a collapsible wooden chair and hugged his overcoat round him as if he were cold. One of his eyes followed the movements of the three women, two elderly and plain, one young and not so plain, around the room. The other eye, the glass one, was still. The three women hated Katz, they had been busy hating him for the last half hour. As they passed him, carrying files, trays of correspondence, to their desks, or on their way out to the washroom with face towels and soap, they skirted his legs and clicked their teeth, loathing him. When the porter in the blue uniform came in with their mid-morning tea and his usual cheerful cry of 'Well, ladies, tea up!' his face froze at the sight of Katz. When Mr Williams, from the overseas department, came in to chat and borrow a file he stared at Katz and went out without a word. When young Gladys from the typing pool drifted in to check on her horoscope in Miss Graham's *Women and Fireside* she only peeped in at the door and, seeing Katz, decided it was an inauspicious moment for those born, as she had been, under Capricorn, and departed. The happiness of Mr Porcher's guardians, as these three women were, had been given the kiss of death by Katz.

'It's no good your waiting. Mr Christopher will tell you just the same when he comes down. He won't see you. You must apply at your local office for a permit.'

Katz said nothing. He took out an old Oxo tin and started to make a cigarette, spilling tobacco dust round the chair.

For a man with two less than the normal amount of fingers he did well.

'What we can't understand,' the eldest woman said, her chin just appearing over a large and primitive typewriter, the rest swathed in three cardigans and an overcoat, 'is how you got past the doorman.'

Katz borrowed a match from the box that was lying on the desk beside Miss Graham's ten Craven A.

'Surely he explained that it was a matter for your local office.'

'Doesn't it say that on the form we sent you?'

'It's not even a matter for head office, let alone the Ministry. Why, it's just like . . . just like changing your ration book.'

'I wouldn't know.' Katz spoke round the corner of his lighted match. 'I never changed a ration book.'

The three women looked at him in silence, horror-struck. Then they gave him up, with one accord their typewriters started thundering. Their galloping fingers, the keys crashing in triplicate, would have drowned any further attempt at conversation. It seemed, though, that Katz still had something to communicate; he left his chair and sidled up to Miss Graham; she kept her eyes steadfastly in front of her, jabbing back the carriage of her typewriter viciously as she came to the end of a line. He spoke, but was inaudible; he went on speaking and the ghastly, unpardonable sentence reached her through the din.

'Sorry to ask you, Miss. Trouble with the bladder ever since North Africa.'

'Second on the right down the passage.'

'Thanks.'

Katz left temporarily. Miss Graham was still scarlet when Mr Christopher, a perfectly charming young man in a blue suit and Old Bedalian tie, glided into the room. The typewriters stopped, six eyes regarded him with adoration.

'The chief's back,' he said. 'He's got five minutes before his next appointment. And the extraordinary thing is –'

'What?'

'He wants to see him.'

'Really!' the eldest guardian pouted, the colour rising in her neck, 'it's too bad for the chief. There ought to be some law passed, there really did. He's just at the mercy of any cranky constituent who likes to come and waste his time.'

'He's too good to these people, that's what he is. They take advantage of him.'

'Just because they voted for him they think that gives them the right –'

'Yes, but where is he? The chief wants him sent in right away.'

'He's . . .' But Miss Graham was spared the indignity of the explanation by the reappearance of Katz in the doorway. His home-made cigarette, although still in his mouth, had gone out and there was a cheerful glint in his good eye.

'This way,' said Mr Christopher, and took Katz out of the room.

'Never come here again!' said Porcher, when he and Katz were alone. 'See that? Never!' He talked in a whisper from behind his desk and his colour was bad. Katz relit the damp cigarette from a table lighter shaped like a golf ball.

'I only had a message. You didn't want it left with the girls outside, did you?'

'Tell me,' Porcher said, 'and get out.'

'Kennet's not ready. He wants another week.'

'He can't have it.'

'Yes he can. You know he can.'

'All right. But tell him when you see him –'

'You'd better keep quiet,' Katz said. 'You've got nothing to say to him. He'll contact me when he's ready.'

'All right. Now get out, blast you.'

'I'm going.'

'And hear what I say. Never come here again. Ring me when you're ready.'

Porcher buzzed and Mr Christopher reappeared. 'Show this gentleman out, will you, Christopher?'

'All right, sweetheart,' said Katz, 'I'll find my way.' He stamped his cigarette end into the carpet and went out. The expression in both his eyes was now the same.

Seton walked through the morning West End pleased with his independence. It was after ten o'clock and most people were at work, only the barrow boys, suburban housewives on shopping expeditions with their youngest children, chorus girls on their way to auditions, the more hopeful prostitutes and the poet Seton were about on the streets. The sun shone on Tottenham Court Road, glinted in the mirrors of mahogany bedroom suites, on the piles of glossy magazines in the bookshops, on the earliest, sporting editions of the evening papers and on the two negroes in purple suits standing by the entrance to the underground station. Over the rattle of the traffic, the cries of the street vendors and the bay of a trumpet played by an elderly white haired man in the gutter, a curious high-pitched noise could have been heard by those who passed nearest to Seton. Fat, untidy, glassy eyed and only partially shaved, with his overcoat flapping and a silk scarf about his neck, Seton appeared to be fired with some inward jollity. He was singing.

' "Ye Banks and Braes o' bonny Doon . . .",' piped Seton as he rattled down the moving staircase of the underground, ' "Oh why so something all wi' care . . .".' When the train arrived he got in, smiling jovially round the compartment. He selected, with the care of a connoisseur selecting a cigar, the prettiest girl in the carriage to sit opposite, and fell to a close scrutiny of her. The scrutiny, as always, somewhat saddened him. However, he found even the bitterness, the certainty that it would all end with a view of the backs of her nylon stockings as she got out at Warren Street, almost pleasurable.

The girl, catching sight of the moist gaze of Seton round the corner of her *Daily Mirror*, did get out and was replaced by an elderly Rabbi in dark glasses. Seton turned up the collar of his coat and the song died on his lips. Seton the debonair, the gorgeous cosmopolitan, the snapper up of chorus girls, proceeding along the Northern line as Diaghileff had rolled, in his special coach, from Berne to Monte Carlo, disappeared. Now he was Seton the inconspicuous stranger on the Trans-Siberian Railway, the anonymous passenger being smuggled through to Switzerland. He was Seton the man of action.

By the time the train came to a stop he had, as much as possible, neutralized his reactions. He even blamed himself for the parts he had played in the train. Sobered, and with a new purpose, he walked round the corner from the underground station into Godiva Crescent.

The wind whipped him after the warm, rubbery air of the underground. His overcoat spread and the legs of his trousers were flattened against his shins. Children playing on the pavement jumped out of the way of the approaching fat man and then tittered at him from the road. Their derisive eyes, peeping at him from over the hands they clamped to their mouths, stung Seton like the wind; once again his mood changed; he was angry. He mounted the steps of Godiva Crescent, pulling the skirts of his overcoat round him with dignity. Looking down into the basement he saw a woman sitting by a kitchen table breast-feeding a child. He turned away abruptly, pushed open the front door and walked upstairs.

Urquhart took a clean sheet of paper. He had drawn, over the other, a series of whales spouting in a stormy sea. On this sheet he would really begin. He looked at the paper and hated it. He didn't want to write, but wanted passionately to have written, a book. He would have liked to have been a writer who never had to write; gift copies, advertisements, reviews, all these would have made him deeply and permanently happy. If only he could make a start. He felt sure, once he started, that the words would flow from him, certain that his life with its school-days, experiences in the

Fire Service, three fully consummated love affairs, would provide startling and original material for a series of full length novels. His pen hovered over the paper, took courage and descended. Rapidly, with certainty and control, he began to draw another whale.

The door clicked behind him. Urquhart threw down his pen, hastily covered up the whale and turned round angrily. If Sylvia had brought that brat up when she knew he must have quiet . . . In the doorway, however, a fat man in a scarlet scarf calmed him with a raised hand, the gesture of a colonial bishop silencing a restless negro congregation.

'I'm not disturbing you, my friend?'

'Well, as a matter of fact, you are,' Urquhart said indignantly.

'I must apologize. I was looking for a young friend. Kit Kennet.'

'He's not here.'

'I know. I've been to his room. Can you tell me, my good friend, when he is expected back?'

'No, I'm afraid I can't.' Urquhart looked pointedly back to his paper, turned it over. Seton approached and gripped the back of his chair.

'Charming. Charming drawings. You make a study of marine life?'

'No, damn you. I'm a novelist.'

'You're a writer? Then you'll know my work. I am the poet Seton.'

Urquhart looked up with respect. 'Seton? Of course, I should have recognized you by your photograph in *New Landscapes*. I am sorry to have been so stupid. You know how devilish this inspiration business is.'

'Naturally.' Seton sat down amiably, his great hands dangling between his legs. 'We must have a good talk about that too sometime. Just at the moment, you don't know where my young friend is, by any chance?'

'He went quite suddenly, a day or two ago. He paid all

his rent. Tell me, do you find poetry easier to write than prose?'

'Oh, yes. It simply pours out of me. Now tell me. Young Kennet, you know him well?'

'Not well, no. He doesn't talk much. Do they pay you well – for poetry, I mean?'

'For poetry, meagrely. Yet you're here all day. You get the telephone messages, see the visitors, things like that, I suppose?'

'Well, I have to, when Sylvia's busy with the baby.'

'My friend, you and I will now go out for a glass of beer. In one of those sad London pubs that smell of the Middle Ages you shall tell me what you know about my young friend.'

Urquhart hastened to put on his tie. He was looking forward, not so much to this unexpected morning drink, as to his drink that evening. He would introduce the matter casually into the conversation – 'Yes, Seton and I were in here this morning. I agree, he is about the best poet writing today. Sad places, these London pubs – they smell of the Middle Ages . . .'

Sylvia looked out of the basement window. She saw her husband's back and something about it told her that he was going out for a drink. The baby on her lap waved its legs gently through the air, rubbed its rose with the back of its fists as she changed it; her mouth was full of safety pins and she leant forward for a better view of Seton, the fat stranger who was taking her husband out.

The sun rose lethargically over Worsfold, as if it hesitated to open its eye on a scene in which there would be nothing new to discover. Mrs Monument, propped on her pillows at the window, consuming her usual mid-morning gin and water and coughing over a cigarette, found the scene of lively interest. She kept up a commentary on it to Sandra Hume who, never having got quite used to this bedroom visiting, was listening uncomfortably.

'Extraordinary odd chap, the old sky pilot,' Mrs Monument was saying as the vicar, wearing a stained cassock and carrying his washing in a large brown paper parcel, emerged from the Post Office. 'He'll never retire or die, I suppose. We'll never get anyone who can put a bit more ginger into the services. Looks so shockingly bad to have a vicar who carts his own washing about like that. Really, your husband ought to do something about that moustache . . . Heavens, what does Peggy think she's bought? No, there she is, just coming out of the shop now. I must say, she looks older every day. My dear, what is she carrying? No, it's not, yes, it's a box of those lavender roots Figgis has been trying to sell off for years. They'll never grow. Dear, do run down and tell her she's wasted her money. No, don't bother now – look at this, just look at it, I ask you! Mrs Seebohm. Seebum I call her, well, she's got enough of it, hasn't she? I know I'm dreadful. But honestly, what a thing to ride, and in trousers too. What on earth is it, a bicycle, a motor bike? I suppose it's a sort of cross between the two, like a mule. Oh, do look, Sandra! Get up and look, child, it's gone phut and the bloody woman can't get it to go again. Do you know she once came to the house and had the cheek to throw herself at Gerry? I do hate her so. Now she's pushing it. She'll have to push it all the way up to Thomson's, and if he mends it for her I'll never speak to him again. Look, Sandra, she's kicking it! Oh, damn, it's started . . .'

Mrs Seebohm, a dubious but cheerful widow, lived in a cottage outside Worsfold, a cottage that the County all found much too comfortable. She seemed content to entertain the local farmers, for whom she always had a bottle of whisky, and, admitting her terror of horses, used for transport the mechanized bicycle to which Mrs Monument objected.

'Now she's stopped again. She's talking to the padre. Who does she think she is, the lady of the manor? Perhaps she wants to put up the banns again. Now she's off. Here comes my brother with his Sealyham. Going to the post. I can't imagine who he writes to. When we were children, Sandra dear, he was always answering advertisements for free samples and things, perhaps he still does. You know – dreadful stuff to put on his face, and things to stop the palms of his hands from sweating. Even after he went to Sandhurst, I remember, they still went on coming. And here's Rolley on his horse – ugly looking brute, the horse I mean. And look, Sandra! Look! I knew something nice was going to happen today. He's got forty-eight hours, here's the car –!'

A red M.G. turned in the road in front of the house and stopped. Kit got out. He walked into the hall and found a letter addressed to Mrs Monument. He put it in his pocket. Upstairs, she turned to him, her eyes wet.

'That car hasn't gone since –'

'I know. I've been fixing it. It's an extravagant little car on petrol, but it goes.'

'Gerry had it for his twenty-firster. He taught me to drive it too.'

'You can drive it now, so long as you drive slowly.'

'Kit, that terrible woman, Mrs Seebohm – on her machine, did you see her?' Mrs Monument was smiling again, rubbing the tops of her arms with her hands at the awfulness of the woman.

'I saw her. Is she terrible?'

'Oh, Kit, of course she is. The woman had the cheek to set her cap at Gerry once, in this very house, too. Of course he just laughed at her. "Glamour Boy", that's what she used to call him. Can you think of anything so awful?'

'No.' Kit stretched out his legs and crossed them. The poor bitch with her bronze hair and green trousers probably was awful. So was Katz with his glass eye and so, in his day, was Gerry Monument. So was Kit Kennet. He stretched out his legs and waited. Soon he would have finished what he had to do here and he could get out of the village, back to the awful world where he belonged.

Mrs Monument continued her inspection of the street. A maid brought in coffee for Kit and Sandra, with a plate of digestive biscuits. Sandra sat farther forward on the edge of her chair and peeped at Kit as if he were a fascinating but dangerous animal that she had been taken to see at the Zoo. She held her saucer in one hand and looked at him over the edge of her coffee cup. She was interested in men in the way that children are interested in animals, remotely, nervously, profoundly. Hitherto they had fallen for her into two classes, her own and the rest. Her own wore tweed caps, laughed loudly and vacantly and met up with you at point-to-points. It was possible if one was the type, to go off the rails with them, to embark, if some of her girl friends were to be believed, on a series of flirtations in motor cars, good times at hunt balls or even illicit weekends. The rest of mankind kept garages or delivered the bread or served in the Bank and, although sometimes unaccountably attractive, naturally could not be thought of in that sort of way. Into what class, she was trying to decide, did Kit fall, with his town clothes, his white shirt and dark tie, the wrist watch which he always wore with the watch on the inside of his wrist. She had never heard him laugh, he appeared to take no interest in horses or chickens, most extraordinary of all he seemed not even to resent the Government. Anxiously, she tried to incorporate him among the people she knew.

'Mrs Mottram was round last night,' she said. 'She thought you might have been at school with her cousin, Rupert Mottram.'

'I might,' Kit said. 'I could never tell the people I was at school with apart.'

Sandra bit on her digestive biscuit. It was as if a child who had thrust a precious piece of bun through the bars to an admired leopard had been greeted with a show of claws. Conversation with Kit, she reluctantly decided, was, like feeding these animals, dangerous.

Mrs Monument was smiling to herself. 'You might take me out in the car some time.'

Kit said, 'Of course I will. This afternoon. This morning we have business.' He took a sheaf of papers from his inside pocket. Sandra got up, blushing.

'Shall I . . . ?'

'Don't go, child. It won't take a minute.' Mrs Monument was possessively anxious to keep even the people who interested her least around her. 'What's this all about?'

'We're changing some investments. This one should pay rather well.'

'Is it safe, Kit? That's the point. Is it safe?'

'Safe as anything nowadays.'

'Government stock, that sort of thing?'

For the first time, Sandra saw Kit smile. 'That sort of thing,' he said.

He made a table of magazines for her on the bed and, having found her fountain pen with some trouble, Mrs Monument signed her name with a flourish. At the same time she shivered. The sun had disappeared and the black clouds which had been travelling over the surrounding hills reached Worsfold, giving it its daily dose of rain.

'Damn it,' said Mrs Monument, disappointed. 'Now we shan't be able to go out in the car.'

'I'm afraid after all I shall have to get back to London this afternoon, anyway. I'll be leaving in about half an hour.'

Sandra couldn't tell whether she felt disappointment or relief.

7

Kennet

Kennet pushed away his plate and shifted his body for comfort in the upright Sheraton chair whose slender mahogany seemed almost too frail for him. He had eaten doggedly though his normal breakfast, disregarding the crackling of his wife's cereal, a permanent protest from the other end of the table at the habits of those who start the day with three kippers. Now he prodded tobacco into the bowl of his pipe, having first blown down it with intense preoccupation.

'So isn't it wonderful news?'

'What wonderful news?'

'I knew you hadn't been listening.' She folded up the letter, put away the glasses she used for reading. 'Mac-Andrew's prepared to take Kit on.'

'The question is,' Kennet said, 'is Kit prepared to take on Mac-what's-his-name. Or am I? How much did you say?'

'Five or six guineas a visit – I forget. It'll take time, of course. He'll have to go five times a week for at least a year. But Kit wants to get adjusted, I know he does. Now he'll have someone he can really talk to.'

'He could talk to me, for a reasonable charge.'

'Oh, you're so stupid!' She pushed the letter back into the envelope with an unrestrained gesture of annoyance. 'You don't seem to *want* to understand. Of course he couldn't talk to you. He's jealous of you. That's the whole trouble.'

'Jealous?' Kennet raised an eyebrow. 'Why?'

His wife let out her breath despairingly, her words came out on the last deflation, as if she were a competent governess explaining an obvious fact to a very backward child. 'Because you're married to me, of course.'

Kennet lit his pipe carefully, considering this. 'You think Kit,' he asked, 'would like to be married to you?'

His wife's hands opened. 'Naturally. Now don't be tiresome about it, will you? You know Kit's been maladjusted, he never wants to come and see us, keeps everything to himself, makes a mystery of everything. Now we can really do something for him.'

Kennet watched his match burn to an end on his plate, then he said, 'Don't you think it's natural, that people should avoid their parents, I mean? Part of the process of growing up. I know I did.'

She sighed at him again. 'You're so complacent. You don't want Kit to grow up like you, do you?'

'Don't I? I suppose I don't.'

'There's no reason at all why there shouldn't be a properly adjusted relationship between him and ourselves. There's no reason why he should live away from home in that squalid room or know those boring Urquharts or hide himself away from us like he does. MacAndrew can turn him into a completely integrated character in a year or so.'

Kennet got up and crossed to the window. His wife stared angrily at his broadly sceptical back. 'I'll make Kit go to MacAndrew,' she said. 'I'll make him go.'

'You can't.' He turned round slowly. 'No one can make Kit do anything. Whatever it is he's finding out, he's got to find it out alone.'

'Everyone who knows anything about psychiatry, everyone who *is* anything at all nowadays, thinks MacAndrew's wonderful. If he's no good for Kit, how do you explain that?'

His hand was on top of the window. He was frowning. 'It might be faith healing. The trouble is, Kit's got no faith.'

'Then you admit he needs healing? That he's sick?'

'Sick?' He shrugged away the word, suggesting to him as it did all that he most hated: curtained rooms, the smell of ether, bustling nurses and the haggard, beseeching faces of the ill. 'Sick? I don't know about that.'

'You wouldn't know. You don't know your own son. You know nothing, nothing about anyone!' She was whispering at him furiously, her voice muted out of consideration for Sophy, her lips drawn back contemptuously on her teeth. 'You know nothing about people!'

'That's probably true.'

'Why don't you do something about it, then – learn something from men like MacAndrew? He's studied behaviour patterns for six years in a Vienna clinic –'

'Well , you know,' he stood in front of her, puzzled by the sharp piercing of her dislike as a bull is puzzled by the pain of the picador's dart. 'Well, you know, I've studied behaviour patterns for thirty years in a solicitor's office.'

'And you've learnt nothing new, nothing new at all. You're stupid and complacent and old-fashioned and dull! Dull, do you hear? Don't touch me!' She shook his hand furiously off her shoulder. He was standing close to her.

'I expect you're right about me,' he said. 'And maybe you're right about MacAndrew. After all, there may have been a Flood and a Noah's Ark and an Immaculate Conception, we can't prove there wasn't. Only leave Kit alone for the moment. He'll be all right.'

'All right? You've no imagination, that's the trouble. Don't you realize? Can't you see' – her face turned up to him bitterly – 'how boring and commonplace you must look to Kit?'

His hand dropped. His pipe had gone out and he put it in his pocket. 'Goodbye,' he said. 'I must go to work.'

She did not answer. He left the room in silence, shutting the door carefully behind him. In the hall he met Sophy; her eyes were bright with interest as she handed him his hat.

His office had, as always, a soothing effect on Kennet.

He liked the Victorian ugliness of the furniture, the neat competence of the filing cabinets, the view of trees in the square through the high Georgian windows. He sat down at his desk and swivelled himself round thoughtfully in his chair. Opposite him was a misty, full-length photograph of his wife in her presentation dress, her clear, contemptuous features merging into the ostrich feathers and the pearly aureole of light cast round her by the Court photographer. How long ago was it, he wondered, that she had started to hate him? He leaned forward for the photograph and put it in a drawer. There would probably be no separation, no divorce, but that was still no reason why they should have to look at each other all day.

His managing clerk brought him the pile of letters, already opened.

'No answer from Mrs Monument?' he asked.

'Nothing yet, sir.'

'All right. Get through to her on the telephone, will you?'

While his clerk was telephoning he found a packet of tobacco in a drawer, stuffed his pipe. In a moment the small, respectful head reappeared round the door. 'Mrs Monument didn't answer the telephone, sir. I got a message that she was temporarily out. She will ring us back.'

'All right, Harrison. Put her on to me when she comes through.'

When the man had gone he put through another call, this time on his private line. Sylvia, he discovered, could meet him at one. Mrs Monument had not telephoned by the time he left the office.

At lunch time London was bathed in the pale yellow light of a day at the beginning of Spring. The thin warmth was, one felt, temporary; at any moment the grey clouds might be drawn up over the Horse Guards' Parade, hail like grape-shot might rattle down between the pillars of the Athenaeum, the flow of typists, bank clerks and civil servants towards St James's Park might be put down like a revolutionary movement. As it was, the light remained yellow over the water, on the smooth, velvet heads of the ducks, and Buckingham Palace appeared, over the trees, like a country mansion.

Kennet walked over the bridge, his hat in his hand, his head stuck forward, frowning. 'You're young,' he said. 'Do I bore you?'

Sylvia turned her eyes on him slowly. 'Bore me? No.' In fact, nothing seemed to bore her. The whole of life apparently possessed for her a remote and dreamlike interest.

'When you're old,' he said, 'you're accused of boring young men. No one stops to think how young men bore you. The tedium of youth – living through it oneself is bad enough, making all the mistakes a sufficient waste of time, but to have to watch it all being done again, just the same –'

'But with Kit,' Sylvia said, 'you said it wasn't the same.'

'That's right.' He looked at her respectfully. 'He is different, of course. But I bore him, no doubt I do. Just like I bored my father and he bored me.'

'I'm young,' said Sylvia, 'in a way. Do I bore you?'

'No.'

'Why?'

They came to the end of the bridge and walked down the broad lake-side path; the typists opened attaché cases and dived for sandwiches, middle-aged couples sat mysteriously hand in hand, the plain, brown-headed ducks swam energetically after their gorgeous drakes.

'Because you're beautiful,' he said, 'and that's neither young nor old, and always interesting.'

She smiled secretly and put her arm through his. A large man came towards them, surrounded, like a drake, with a flock of hatless, sleek-headed young men in neat suits who jostled for positions near him and listened to his words. His Yorkshire accent boomed out.

'I've got no more economic theory,' he was saying, 'than the man in the street, but what the professors and the pundits can never explain to me is . . .' He saw Kennet and swept off his hat, raising his shaggy eyebrows enquiringly at Sylvia. Kennet bowed his head slightly and they passed by without speaking.

'Who,' Sylvia asked, 'is that appalling man?'

'He's called Porcher. And talking of bores . . . but we won't. Let's have lunch.'

They came out between the naked plane trees of the Mall. Kennet felt the faint warmth of the sun, the more immediate warmth of the woman beside him, and shivered. The sunlight, he seemed to realize, was an illusion, the winter died hard and there was a savage kick in it still.

They had lunch in a restaurant near the park, set between the shops for selling rare fishing equipment and the hat shops which displayed, tentatively and with a horror of seeming ostentatious, one green felt hat on a dusty shelf. Kennet looked round the restaurant unhappily; with its neon lights and aquarium, its swarthy clientele, women in fur coats, men with jewelled tie pins, it seemed wrong and indelicate, a difficult atmosphere in which to celebrate the death of a London winter. He turned to Sylvia.

'How's the baby?'

'He's away. With my mother, in the country.'

'I'm always talking about Kit. Tell me about him. What are his problems?'

She laughed. 'He's too young for them. I don't mind what he does when he grows up.'

'That's what I always said about Kit. Except I'd have hated him to be a parson.'

'Yes. Or a ballet critic.'

He laughed with her. It's a wonderful thing, he thought, how she can warm the atmosphere of this high grade, upper class, highly ruinous cafeteria. He asked, as though it didn't matter to him at all, 'And when's he coming back?'

'Not for a week or two. My husband's going away next weekend to stay with a friend at Cambridge. So I shall be –'

'All alone?'

Her hand was on the table and he took it; as his hand covered hers she looked back at him steadily, remotely, but with a sort of defiance. 'Yes.'

It doesn't matter, Kennet thought, how old or young you are, the feeling is the same with the first woman you meet and the last, the world around you grows dim and disappears in the same way and you feel the same trembling of the stomach as if, with each sharing of pleasure, you were planning to face another death.

That evening Kennet had dinner late and then telephoned twice from the hall of his house. When he had put down the telephone for the second time he sat down on the third stair from the bottom and held the bridge of his nose for a moment, thinking. His wife opened the white sitting-room door and came out into the hall.

'Christopher – what are you doing? What would Sophy think if she saw you sitting there?'

'She'd think I was tired of standing up. She'd be right.'

'Don't be absurd. What were you phoning for?'

'Kit.'

'Why Kit?' She looked down on him, swinging her spectacles in her hand, her mouth tight.

'Perhaps I was wrong this morning. He shouldn't be left alone any longer. I ought to see him.'

She smiled slowly. 'He tells me things occasionally, you know. He's gone to the country.'

'I guessed that. I telephoned the woman he'd been staying with. He left just before lunch.'

'Then he'll be at his room.'

'I telephoned there, too. He's not back and they hadn't heard he was coming.'

He got up slowly and went into the room at the back of the house which he used for working. His wife followed him and leant against the edge of the desk, moving a pile of papers.

'Really, the mess in here. No wonder Sophy can never get in to do it. Did you say a woman?'

'Kit's hostess. She's in her late sixties and usually had too much to drink. This evening she'd had far too much.'

'I can't understand it.'

'Neither can I.' He went over to the window and looked out at the dusk over the urban gardens; the black twigs on the trees were just coming into leaf and a shadowy cat prowled along a wall. There was a man standing in the empty road looking up at the house.

From behind him, his wife said, 'What did you want Kit about? Business?'

'Partly. I wanted to talk to him.'

She laughed, a little puff of humourless laughter. 'How you misunderstand Kit! I believe you'd have done a ridiculous paternal act in your study.'

'I don't understand him. I want to talk to him. After what you said this morning, I've been thinking I've rather failed with Kit. I should have given him something to believe in, even if it was something I didn't believe in myself.'

He turned round into the darkening room. His wife said, 'You've rather failed with a good many things, haven't you? Do you remember that before we were married you wanted to paint?'

'I may still,' he smiled back. 'I may disappear to the South Seas tomorrow.'

'You won't.' Her voice came back at him, clipped and positive. 'You'll go on just as you are. And Kit will go on as he is whatever you say to him.'

'And you?'

He sat down at the desk and ran his fingers along the edge of it. When she answered her voice was only a little less certain. 'I shall go on as I am, of course. I've got all I want here.'

'All you want,' he repeated slowly.

'Of course. I'm not like you, Christopher. I've kept alive.

I've got my friends, interests. I've kept up with what the young are thinking and doing, which is why I've got Kit and you've lost him. I'm sorry to have to say that to you again, but it's true.'

His hand moved along the edge of the desk towards her. When it rested for a moment against her side, she moved away quickly as if she had been stung.

'Yes,' he said. 'You've got a good many friends. You'd better have them all to lunch next Sunday.'

'What do you mean?'

'I've got to go away for the weekend.'

'Work?'

He turned towards the window. 'Not exactly.'

'Perhaps it's just as well. There may be a good many people in on Sunday anyway. They seem to like it here.'

'Particularly when I'm away?'

'I didn't say so.'

When she had left the room he rose and went back to the window. The man in the road, who was thin and had a hat pulled down over one eye, was still watching the house. Kennet opened the window and the man sunk his hands into his pockets and walked away.

Kennet lit and finished a pipe as he looked out. Then he turned back into the room and switched on the light on his desk. It flooded the wall and the one possession which Kennet prized, a framed drawing of a woman with her foot resting on the edge of a hip bath, drying her legs. She appeared to be quite absorbed in the process. Kennet had sometimes wondered who she was, a flower girl perhaps, or an art student, or a singer at a *café chantant*, and he thought that of all the men to whom she had given pleasure in her life to none had she given more pleasure than to the artist who drew her and to Kennet, who had the picture. She also seemed to him the sort of woman on whom a man might put his hand without making her run for the door.

The room had become cold, and he felt a change coming over him. Although he sat down to work, as he always did after dinner, at the pile of papers on his desk, he did so with a curious feeling of detachment. It was as if the life to which he had committed himself was ending, the elaborate performance which had become a second nature to him would soon become unnecessary. It seemed to him that, having lived so long, he had ceased to care, he had suddenly become young again.

He made himself work, however, until after midnight. Then he went to bed and slept soundly and alone. He rang up Godiva Crescent again before breakfast and spoke to Sylvia. He discovered that Kit had not come back. After he had found this out, he said, 'About next weekend. You said you'd be alone. Will you meet me on Saturday morning?'

There was no pause, no hesitation before she answered, 'Yes.'

8

Rolley

At Worsfold, after Kit's departure, the atmosphere slightly
relaxed. Sandra Hume, walking her son Nicholas round an
overgrown paddock on his pony, found herself still thinking of Kit but forgetting, confusedly, his appearance. Her
husband Vernon had written to the Governor of Rhodesia
about the prospects of immigration and lay about the house
waiting for a reply. Peggy had her cousin Nora, a fifteen
year old girl whose parents were in India, to stay; Rolley
eyed the girl critically and then spent most of his time out
of the house. The widow Mrs Seebohm, whom Mrs
Monument had derided from her bedroom window, was
often seen in the pub with a young officer from the aerodrome and had replaced Kit as a topic of conversation.
About the middle of the week Rolley had a letter from his
bank manager. Mrs Monument saw no one for three days
and drank more than she had before.

She woke up on the morning of the third day with a
curious feeling of peace, as if she had woken up in a vast,
empty ballroom where she had fallen asleep among a crowd
of noisy dancers. The night before she had finished a bottle
of gin in her bedroom with the wireless blaring and the
furniture rocking in front of her dazzled eyes. Now everything was still and silent. She stretched her old hands, with
their loose, brown, papery skin, in front of her on the sheet
and opened her eyes slowly. She decided to get up and do
some gardening, an activity by which she hoped to show,
as she appeared in her much observed and exposed front

garden, that she was taking her place in the County again at last.

She got up and pulled her clothes on, finally impaling a floppy summer hat on her grey head with as much casualness as one would spike a bill on a nail in the wall. As she glanced at herself in the long mirror in her bedroom she found herself wearing a tweed skirt, a low cut silk blouse, a string of shell beads, woollen stockings and bedroom slippers. Undismayed, she wandered downstairs, equipped herself with leather gauntlets, secateurs and a tiny, ornamental straw basket that had once come with an Easter egg. She then went out of doors.

The sunlight, that morning, gave the garden a curious enamelled brightness. Unusually, for the moment, the sky was blue. Above the distant but still active aerodrome the white trails of Meteors hung in the sky and slowly dispersed with the wind. Mrs Hume-Monument surveyed her rock plants from what seemed to her very far away. The minute, greenish-grey vegetation which covered the boulders of the rockery might have been a primeval forest growing on the moon, seen through a telescope at Greenwich. She drew her secateurs and ambled towards a standard rose; apparently confused as to the seasons of the year, she began relentlessly to prune.

After half an hour's work she went in for a pair of sun glasses and came out with her eyes hidden behind gigantic black saucers, looking more frail and insect-like than before. She avoided the standard rose and knelt by her border to weed. She had always been a good weeder and the gestures came automatically, her fingers broke up the grey, chalky earth and pulled out grass and groundsel with energy and skill.

After a little while she sat back on the lawn, tired. The daisies were just appearing and she picked some and tried to thread them into a chain. Her hand was trembling too much for that, so she contented herself with laying them out in a circular pattern on the grass. Then she went back into the house to find a cigarette.

When she came out again she was surprised by a hammering from the garage. She walked round the house and opened the garage door. The place was gloomy and she had to take off her sun glasses to see who was there.

'Rolley!'

Rolley squirmed out from under the car, red in the face and greasy. He stood up slowly, like a schoolboy who had been caught trying to crawl into a circus tent.

'Rolley!' Her indignation turned to amusement. 'Rolley, what do you think you're doing?'

'Oh, hello, Aunt.' Rolley sounded as cheerful as he could. 'Just giving the old bus a going over for you. Tuning her, you know.'

'Thank you, but Kit did that for me before he left.'

'I know.' Rolley kicked viciously at a tyre. 'I know he did. Frankly, I'm not sure that young Kennet knows his way about cars. I just wanted to check up again on her for you.'

'It was a nice thought, Rolley, but I'm sure Kit knew just what he was doing. Now come and wash your face and I'll give you a drink.'

'I was just going to finish tuning –'

'I told you I was grateful. I like its tune as it is. Come along – I know you'll join me.'

Rolley threw the rag he had been wiping his hands with down on the ground and followed her into the house. He washed in the downstairs lavatory, where he had a chance of reading a framed copy of *Invictus*, and joined his aunt in the sitting room. She had put on her glasses again and taken off her hat.

'Up to the pretties, will you? You know, Rolley, this work doesn't really suit you.'

'As a matter of fact, I know a good deal about cars. Before the war I knew a fellow who used to race at Brooklands.'

'Not working on cars. Working on old women. You haven't got the knack.'

'Really, Aunt!' Rolley, who had his glass on the way to his mouth, went red in the face and put it down again on the table. Although Mrs Hume-Monument did not see it, there was more in his face than embarrassment. There was also hatred.

'Gerry had the knack. So has Kit Kennet. I always know what they're after, but it's worth it, to be with them. Unfortunately nothing's worth being with you.'

'I don't understand.' Rolley stepped towards the old woman, her eyes masked, who lay back in the big chintz arm chair. 'If you're saying I've got nothing in common with that young twister Kennet, I'm very flattered –' He paused a moment and went on, 'As for Gerry, he's . . .' Rolley bit back the word. Angry as he was, he couldn't yet bring himself to say the word 'dead'.

'Different?' Mrs Hume-Monument smiled. 'Perhaps he is. But he and Kit have something in common, nevertheless. I'm only saying you shouldn't try to beat them at their own game.'

'What did young Kennet come here for? Did he make you sign anything? What did he make you do?' Rolley's voice was very quiet; he looked down at her from the corners of his eyes.

The thin hand came out for the library book. Mrs Hume-Monument pushed her glasses up on her forehead and started to read. The audience was over. 'That,' she said, 'is not your affair, Rolley. I suggest you go home and continue to act as an outraged and helpless relative. Don't ever try to do me little kindnesses again,' she lifted her glass and blinked at him over it, 'because it doesn't suit you, and I don't like it.'

As Rolley left the house he ran into Sandra who, on the express instructions of her husband, was bringing her aunt a bunch of flowers.

'She's been drinking again,' he muttered. 'You can't do

anything for her. Started to overhaul her car for her, but she wouldn't have it. One of these days she's going to wake up and find out what's coming to her. Then she'll really need a drink.'

But what had finally happened between Kit Kennet and Mrs Monument was not known to Rolley until the next afternoon, and then his fury at the stupid, infantile, drunk old woman, which had long been festering, exploded.

He had taken his wife's cousin Nora out hunting, and Sandra and her child Nicholas were expected to tea. By tea-time Rolley was hating the girl Nora whose forehead was still red from scrubbing away the blood with which she had been smeared, and whose eyes were still ecstatic. Rolley had come down to tea in his shirt-sleeves and riding breeches and boots. The ginger hair on his chest showed between the buttons of his shirt and he wore no tie. He behaved rudely in order to emphasize his virility and healthy weariness. In fact he felt sick.

Opposite him at the tea table his wife Peggy poured the tea. Beside her, Sandra tried to prevent Nicholas, who had not been out hunting, from putting his fingers into the sugar bowl.

'Had a good day, dear?' Peggy asked.

'Rotten.'

'Oh, Uncle Rolley, how could you say . . .' Nora, tapping the top of a boiled egg, rebuked him gently.

'I say it was rotten.'

'Rotten,' said Nicholas. 'Rotten. Rotten. Rotten.' He bit a hole in his bread-and-butter and putting his eye to it, peeped through at Rolley.

'Sandra, do shut the child up.'

Rolley tore open two letters which had come by the after-noon post. They were both bills, and he pushed them into his breeches pocket shamefully, almost as though they had been love letters he didn't want his wife to see. Peggy, who knew exactly what they were, carefully poured out another cup of tea.

'Be quiet, Nicholas dear.'

'I'm not Nicholas dear. I'm Nicky darling. Aren't I, Mummy? I'm darling, darling Nicky.'

'Needs a good tough prep. school, that child. They'd beat some of the nonsense out of him.'

'I don't like you!' Nicholas waved emphatically at his uncle. His hair, during the gesture, came out of its slide and fell over his face in a coquettish manner. Sandra combed it back with the slide.

'You enjoyed the day, anyway, Nora?' Peggy asked.

'Oh, It was lovely, Aunt Pegs. I jumped – oh, I never knew I could jump like it!'

Rolley had seen her, the little fool, go over a loose wall with a ditch on the other side, riding, scarlet in the face, like a girl possessed. He had come after her and his horse had lifted its head and side-stepped, showing a frightened eye and yellow teeth, and all of a sudden Rolley had gone sick inside, dreading the pain from a fractured rib or collar bone; his hands had broken out in sweat and his feet had gone cold. There had been no one near him and he had pulled round and ridden for the gap. He thought no one had seen him until he saw Barbara Underwood, whom he had taken home in his car from the last hunt ball, grinning at him as they rode into the next covert.

'What's the matter, Rolley?' she had asked. 'Haven't you paid up the life insurance?'

And then the damn' kid Nora had ridden up beside them. 'Isn't it super jumping, Uncle Rolley? I remembered all you'd taught me . . .'

Now she said again, 'Did you see me go over that wall, Uncle Rolley? Was I right?'

'You held his head too hard.'

But the girl wasn't listening, she was spooning out her egg and nothing that anyone could say could spoil her day. She would never have believed that Rolley had been glad to dismount. His horse had shied again at a bus on the road back, he had heard the slither of gravel under its hooves and once again his palms had begun to sweat. Up in his room he had washed his face and finished his flask.

'Nicholas!'

The child had slid off its chair and was running at an extraordinary rate round the table.

'Really, I'm sorry about this, Peggy. Nicholas, now you know it's naughty!' Sandra stood up ineffectually, her arms spread out. As the child came round for the third time Rolley put out his boot and Nicholas fell, howling in an ecstasy of grief. Sandra gathered him up and fed him on her knee with strips of bread-and-butter.

'Rolley!' Peggy protested from behind the teapot.

'He made me do it! He made me fall down!'

'You're a silly cry-baby,' Nora said calmly, scraping out her egg, for Rolley was still her hero who had taught her to jump.

'These meals!' Rolley pushed his chair back and lit a cigarette, ostentatiously starting to read the farming paper that had come with his letters.

When silence had been restored, Sandra embarked timidly on a general conversation. She valued these afternoons when she came to gossip with her sister, and neither Rolley's surliness nor Nicholas's hysteria was going to cheat her of her pleasure. 'Really,' she said, 'Aunt Hester was just too marvellous the other morning. She was looking out of her window and making such remarks about everyone –'

'About us?' asked Peggy, who remembered the face she had seen looking down on her as she came out of the shop, having made purchases she now realized to have been unwise.

'Oh, not you. I don't think so.' Sandra blushed and hurried on. 'But that Mrs Seebohm, the things she called her. Apparently Mrs Seebohm had something to do with Gerry, so Aunt Hester hates her, I couldn't say why, really . . .'

'Something to do with Gerry!' Rolley put down his paper. 'She doesn't know the half of it.'

'Ssh . . .' Peggy's eye flickered towards Nora, the girl to whom it must not be disclosed that men were capable of becoming attached to other creatures besides horses.

But Rolley blundered on. To do so gave him some relief, the same relief that he had felt when the child had fallen over his boot. 'Gerry spent his leaves up with La Seebohm, times when he told his mother he couldn't get down.'

'Nora,' Peggy said, 'go out to the kitchen and get us some more hot water, there's a dear.'

Realizing that she was being dismissed, Nora rose sulkily and went out with the hot water jug, walking with exaggerated slowness and banging against the furniture as she steered herself towards the door.

Before she was out of the room, Rolley had gone on, 'Didn't you know, Sandra, it was the scandal of the district? I believe Gerry had a fight with some farmer lout about her, anyway he was always there and they used to go up to London together, too. Even his last weekend —'

'No, Rolley,' Peggy protested. 'You don't know that's true.'

'Of course I know. Everyone in Worsfold knows, except his mother, of course. I'll tell you what happened, Sandra. He was supposed to come on leave to Aunt Hester, but at the last moment he spent his weekend with the Seebohm wench instead, over-spent it, it seems. On the last night, when he was due on an operation at midnight, he was still three parts out at Seebohm's. It seems some pal of his drove over there to dig him out and haul him back to the 'drome. Apparently he was still very lit up and insisted on driving, anyway he piled up the car, shook up his friend pretty badly and killed himself. That was the end of Gerald Monument, dead in the course of duty. Of course they wrapped it up for his mother. Made it sound pretty good.'

There was a shocked, uneasy silence. Nora came back with the hot water and flopped into her chair. She was flushed and determined, as if saying, I am fifteen now, I have watched a fox being torn to pieces, I know what it is that makes women like me so irritable once a month, I stay up to supper, I am not going to be excluded from this conversation.

Sandra asked quietly, 'And Mrs Seebohm's never told Aunt Hester how . . . how Gerry died?'

'Of course not.'

'I think that's jolly decent of her. If she knew, I don't think Aunt would be so – so beastly about her.'

'Seebohm soon found comfort elsewhere. Comforts for the troops, that's what we used to call her.' Rolley crackled his paper and retired behind it again.

Desperately, his wife changed the conversation. Her voice was controlled, too controlled, and there was a hint of white round her mouth. 'And tell us, Sandra, what else did Aunt Hester say?'

But Sandra was thoughtful. 'Oh, nothing else, specially. She stopped then. Kit Kennet wanted her to sign some paper and she –'

'Yes?' Rolley bundled his paper on the floor beside him, leant forward. 'Yes, what did she do? Did she sign?'

Sandra looked up, startled. 'Yes. Yes, I think she signed.'

'Careful, Rolley!' In standing up, Rolley had spilt his tea. The brown stain spread over the lace cloth; Peggy put a plate under it to keep it from the mahogany.

'The little rat!' Rolley shouted. 'I told you it was about time Aunt Hester knew a thing or two! She was fooled by that good-for-nothing son of hers, and now she's fooled by that slimy young Kennet. And us, what about us, we don't get a look in! It's time she learnt a thing or two about both of them, she's been taken in enough. It seems I'm the one to tell her what's been going on!'

Nora's mouth opened slowly as Rolley slammed out of the room. Peggy's hand stroked her knife and Sandra found herself blushing.

'Kit,' she started to say, 'Kit's not . . .'

The brown stain was noticed by Nicholas. 'Ucky!' he

shouted. 'Ucky Uncle Rolley! Uncle Rolley's been a bad ucky boy . . .!'

But Rolley was out of the house, striding towards Mrs Hume-Monument who lay in bed, tired of the garden again, alone, drinking gin, with the portrait of her son.

9

The End of an Illusion

That night, in the country round Worsfold, the moon came out early and gave to the narrow roads and sweeping hills a grey, unconvincing light. The village was a quiet cluster of buildings over which the clouds sailed like battleships, blotting out a house at a time. Now and again a door opened, letting out a bar of light and a whiff of music from a wireless programme. At half-past ten the pub door opened and the last drinkers dribbled into the street. Doors banged and then it was silent again. An oil lamp went swinging up a field as a woman was sent out to shut up the hens. A dog was turned out for the night and yapped a little before it went to sleep. Over a piece of waste ground an owl shrieked as it dropped on a mouse. But these sounds were all part of the silence.

It was broken by a crash as a bottle, thrown from Mrs Monument's window, fell into the gutter and broke. She stood alone in the middle of her bedroom. She was dressed in a pair of trousers and an overcoat, a blue scarf round her neck. She had drunk herself, for the moment, sober. It was a long time since Rolley had left.

Under the heavy overcoat she seemed very fragile. Her face was pale and her thin fingers trembled as she carefully made up her mouth. The gin she had drunk had made her peaceful and content, happy and clear in the head. She had thrown the bottle as a gesture of annoyance at her idiotic cousin. Why, in God's name, she asked herself, did he think she would have minded? Why had Gerry thought she'd have minded? Of course, she'd have sworn a bit, kicked up a fuss, said the sort of things she had said out of the window that morning, but in her heart, if he was doing what he wanted, she would not have minded.

Rolley was an ass. What did it matter to her, his mother, if Gerry died covered with glory or drunk in a ditch? Did it matter if he was shot as a hero or a deserter? He was dead, wasn't he? Dead. Dead. She repeated the word slowly, respectfully. It was the first time, since she had heard the news, that she had dared to say it, even to herself. He was dead, poor Gerry, and would have to go from her, his mother, and from his mistress. They would have to let him go.

She breathed out, relieved. It was as if some penance, some miserable vow to which she had been adhering all these years, were suddenly discharged. She had fed her child, taught him to walk and speak, clothed him, cared for him, and now it was all over. He had grown up and died. That was all that was expected of her, or of him.

She smiled a little as she thought of Rolley, the stuttering, angry civilian, appalled at Gerry's behaviour. He should at least have died like a gentleman. Poor Rolley. How could you be born like a gentleman, or make love like one, or least of all die like one? The moments of life which were of importance were, all of them, private, unconventional, unconsidered. So had been Gerry's death.

Now that she knew the truth she could, so it seemed to her, get on with her life and bring it towards its conclusion. It was as if a gramophone which has stuck for a long time at a crack in a record and has repeated an endless, pointless phrase, had been jolted and the needle had begun, at last, to move towards the end of the melody.

And so it was that for the first time since her son's death Mrs Monument saw outside herself, indistinctly at first, like a dreamer awakening to the reality of a strange room, and then more clearly. She realized that the woman she had laughed at from her window had known the truth all along and had kept the secret as Gerry, foolishly, had wanted it kept; as presumably it would always have been kept if Rolley had not been scared of a jump or cheated out of a few pounds. She pushed her powder compact into her overcoat pocket and said aloud, 'Poor woman.'

She wanted to see Mrs Seebohm, and now she knew everything, she felt there was no time to waste. She went out of the house into the moonlight; she had forgotten to change her bedroom slippers and they made little noise on the gravel. She pulled open the garage doors and got into the red sports car. Her fingers were trembling as they groped for the ignition switch; her foot came off the clutch too quickly, the car shot back and grazed the garage door as she turned; with considerable effort she swung it out into the road. She drove out of the village, driving, as she had seen Gerry drive, with her foot flat down on the accelerator.

The headlamps gilded the stone walls, flashed against the darkened cottage windows and thrust into the hedges, lighting up, for a second, the sharpness of every twig. The faster she drove the more motionless, the more at peace Mrs Monument felt. The wind bathed her forehead and lifted her thin hair; she was a child on a swing, a girl on her first pony, a young woman on a toboggan rushing to meet the blinding, white snow. She drove, as Gerry had, with the dashboard lights on and their greenness showed up her face, her features appeared delicate, unanxious, old, against the blackness which rushed beside her. Her fingers barely touched the wheel. The road in front was a white worm endlessly consumed. The car swept up to the summit of the hill, it seemed to have enough speed to drive into the dark sky that surrounded it. At the top of the hill the road dipped and twisted, and the back wheels skidded as she turned. Her foot groped for the brake, twisted in the loose slipper, on to the accelerator. The stone bank of the road leapt towards her. Mrs Monument was still smiling.

'What is it, Peter?' Mrs Seebohm, in her dressing gown,

looked up from the hearthrug at the young officer from the aerodrome who, with his jacket unbuttoned, had been over to shut the window.

'Nothing. I thought I saw a car coming down the road. Were you expecting anyone?'

'This time of night?'

'Must have been going the other way, I suppose, or they'd be here by now.'

'Did you see the lights?'

'Seemed like it. Can't have been, though. Cars don't suddenly disappear.'

'Of course not. It must have been the moon.' But the cheerful, red-headed woman shivered, as if she had been reminded of something.

10

Faces in a Mirror

'Dead? How can she be dead?' But the distracted, almost deaf, housekeeper had stopped answering, and Kit put the telephone back in the cradle. He was frowning as he slowly found and lit a cigarette. He looked out of the french windows at the garden, bright and vulgar as the photograph on a seed packet, which stretched down to the river. His host, a fat man in shorts and a silk shirt, was polishing the ventilators on a cabin cruiser which was moored within sight of the house.

Kit blinked. It was as if the news he had heard had brought the picture before his eyes into sharper focus. It was also, he thought, as if the news of Mrs Monument's death had made him think of her as a live person for the first time. His stay in Worsfold, his conversation with Katz, this visit to the fat man in his house by the river, the contact for the disposal of the stuff when the deal was completed, might all have been a dream but for the hard, inescapable fact of the old woman's death.

He went out into the garden, still frowning. It wasn't going to make any difference, of course, but he wanted to think it over. He had to move on and think it over. He threw the end of his cigarette into an ornamental lily pond; a china gnome looked up at him with a mild, whimsical rebuke.

He reached the end of the garden and stood in the sun, a pale, thin young man in dark clothes that made no concession to the cheerful riverside Sunday. The fat man on

the boat turned round and saw him. He had small, sus-
picious eyes and beads of sweat stood out on his ginger
moustache.

'Hullo, old man. Soon be time for a snifter.'

'Sorry, I've just had some news. I've got to get back to
Town.'

The man frowned. 'Nothing wrong?'

'The deal's still on, if that's what worries you. But I've
got to get back.'

'Sorry about that.' The man didn't sound too sorry. 'I
could have taken you to a place up river tonight. Decent
sort of hole.' He turned back and polished the ventilator
again.

'I'll get in touch,' Kit said, 'when it's ready to collect.'

'All right, old man, that's understood all right.' He spoke
without turning round. A gramophone started playing
from the other side of the river.

'It won't be long,' Kit said.

'Can't be too soon for me, old man. This waiting's doing
me no good. When it's over, I'm pulling out to France for
a holiday.' He spoke casually, but Kit saw his anxious,
sweating face reflected in the brass he was polishing.

'Don't scare yourself too much,' Kit said. 'You might
drop in the river.'

'As you know,' the fat man said. 'I'm not used to this
sort of deal. I'll be all right, though. Jackie'll drive you to
the station.'

'You'll get used to it. I'll walk.'

Kit went into the shadowy house and collected his suitcase, filling his pocket with cigarettes from the imitation
alabaster box at his bedside. On the lawn in front of the
house a woman in a white dress was lying in a long chair,
listening to a portable radio. She switched off the radio as
he came out of the house and looked after him as he walked
down the gravel path and out of the front gate. Kit did not
look back and, when he was out in the lane that led to the
town and the railway station, he heard the music start again.

He waited half an hour for a slow, Sunday train and sat in a dusty carriage without a corridor smoking the loose cigarettes from his pocket. He got to London and left his case at the station. He had no very clear idea of what he was going to do, or why he was going to do it. It wasn't until he was on an empty bus circling the deserted, Sunday evening streets north of the Park that he clearly realized he was going to see his father.

He got off the bus and started walking, not asking himself why he should be going home, or what he expected from it. The quiet streets, with the couples in stiff, dark clothes coming out of the park, the distant tinny summons to evensong in a neglected church, were heavy with the smell of Sunday. It made Kit shiver. He wanted, perhaps, to reassure his father, to tell him that what had happened at Worsfold wasn't a part of his plan; perhaps he wanted to reassure himself. Whatever the truth was, he hardly knew what he was doing as he walked up the steps and opened the front door with his own latch key.

The hall, as he came in, was very silent. There seemed to be a great emptiness about the house, as if it had been deserted by the people who lived in it. His feet echoed in the hall, and the noise he made surprised him. He pushed open the sitting room door.

'Christopher? Are you back? Kit!' His mother was sitting at a small table playing patience. Her long, manicured hand hovered over a row of cards and then went up to take off her glasses.

'Hullo, Mother.' He came into the room slowly and sat down, searching in his pockets for the last cigarette.

'Kit, you're back! That's wonderful. Did you have a good time? Are you tired?'

'Neither.'

'You must be. And hungry –'

'No, really not.'

'But –'

'I am not hungry.'

'Now I won't ask you anything tonight. Go straight upstairs and I'll get Sophy to bring you something on a tray. In the morning, when you've rested well, we'll have a long talk. There's something I want you to do for me – someone I want you to meet.'

He looked at her blankly, without interest.

'A most wonderful man, Kit.' She got up from the table and came round to sit in front of him on a long, embroidered seat in front of the empty grate. 'A very wise man, darling, he's going to be the most wonderful help to us all.'

'Maybe we need it,' Kit said. 'Is Father in?'

'No. No, he's away this weekend. Some business or other. So lucky you came back just now, when he's away. It would have confused you otherwise, wouldn't it, dearest? I know things have been confusing for you lately.'

'Oh?' He found the cigarette at last, and lit it. 'How do you know that, Mother?'

'Well, you never tell us anything, of course.' Her hands folded and gripped her spectacles. 'You haven't been able to settle down since you left home, have you, Kit dear? But I mustn't worry you tonight, now you're back.'

He didn't answer, but looked round the room as if it were a strange place to him. His mother put a hand on his knee. 'Darling, has something happened? You would tell me, wouldn't you, if something bad had happened?'

He got up and walked away from her, round the room. 'Only one bad thing. A woman I know has died. Killed in a motor accident.'

'Kit –' His mother leant forward. 'Was she a girl you knew – well?'

'She wasn't a girl. She was sixty-five.'

'The woman you were staying with?'

'Yes. Where's he gone?'

'Christopher?' she asked sharply. 'I told you, I don't know.'

He sat down again, looking at her. 'Does he often go away like this?'

'Sometimes. He has business.'

'Do you mind?'

She smiled at him, less anxious now. 'Of course not. Kit, you know how things have been between your father and myself for years. He goes his own way, I go mine. It's a civilized arrangement. It ought to make things easier between you and me.'

'Yes. Perhaps it ought.'

'Did you come here to see him?' She had heard the doubt in his voice, and her question was hard.

'In a way. I thought he might have been trying to get in touch with me. I've been away, as you know, and – that's really why I came.' He was speaking quickly, as if anxious to get her answer. 'Has he been trying to contact me, do you know? Did he say anything about that?'

She looked at him carefully, and then got up and walked to her table, beginning to stack up the cards.

'Kit, I ought to tell MacAndrew – he's the friend I was talking about. Did you come here because you wanted to see your father? Do you still feel – dependent on him?'

Kit said, 'We might have had some business. Was he asking about me?'

'No.' She had made a neat pack which she slid back into a leather card-case. 'No, as a matter of fact, I don't think he asked for you at all.'

There was a silence. Then Kit stood up.

'Dearest, don't worry.' She came and stood close to him again. 'Don't worry about anything. There are so many other people who want to help you. So many people who really care – friends of mine who come to this house, who can be real friends of yours too. Go up and rest now, Kit, that's the best thing. Go and rest.'

'And have something on a tray?' he asked bitterly. 'No, there's a man I must meet. Good-night, Mother.'

'Will you be back later this evening?'

'I don't know. Don't wait up.'

'You'll let yourself in? You have a key?'

'Yes. Good-night.'

So, although Kit went away and the front door clicked after him, Mrs Kennet turned back into the room not completely dissatisfied. Later, she rang for Sophy and made sure that she had aired Kit's bed.

When he got out of the house, Kit drank in air. Although he had told his mother that he had to meet someone, there was no one for him to meet; the point of his sudden journey to London was gone. For the first time in a good many months he walked along the streets for the sake of walking, and not because there was anywhere he had planned to go.

As he walked, he was angry. He dug his hands into his pockets and a sullen rage slowly overcame him. The sky, which was darkening, the streets, which were lighting up, the people who passed him without noticing him, even the beggar who sightlessly rattled a tin box at him or the whore who spoke to him without caring whether he answered her or not, seemed part of a vast indifference. An old woman could kill herself in a motor car, Kit could make his fortune, but his father, casual as the sky or the blank faces of the crowd, wouldn't turn round or notice and, when Kit wanted to see him, he wouldn't be there. He felt like shouting at the strangers in the street, making them at least realize that something unforeseen and remarkable had happened. If I'd murdered her, he thought, he wouldn't have had time to hear how I did it.

He walked with his nostrils stiff with anger, his body aching. He wanted to finish with Katz and Porcher and start something new, something where the risk would be even greater and the stakes higher, something which would make his father and men like him realize that their peaceful, private, painless world had been broken into at last. He walked quickly and his feet rang on the pavements, every footstep was a protest against the silent complacency of the empty streets.

As he came out of the side streets around Piccadilly, he

was soothed by the hooting of traffic, the green and scarlet glare of the lights. He wanted to drink, and he went down the steps of a bar he knew, a small, crowded, rather gloomy bar attached to a theatrical club. As he came in a piano was playing and a young man was singing a sentimental song. It was a low, incomprehensible wail, as tuneless and sexless as the moans of a native woman crouched under the wall of an Eastern town. Kit pushed his way to the bar, deriving a sort of satisfaction from the sight of the men with bow ties and tinted hair, the girls with small, sullen faces and tight trousers. He was glad that the world contained people and things that, he thought, would have appalled his father.

He got to the bar and ordered whisky, looking at the barman with hatred. It came in a small glass; he drank it neat, and it was rather warm. As he lifted the second glass a soft, anxious voice said, 'We've all been looking for you for days.'

It was Seton, his stomach hanging over the top of his trousers, his tie twisted under one ear, his shirt buttons undone and a look of moist curiosity in his eyes.

'Oh, hell,' Kit said. 'Do you have to be here?'

'Always. Seton, Seton, everywhere, and not a drop to drink.' He pushed his empty beer mug along the counter, but Kit disregarded it.

'Buy your own drinks.'

'You're not polite.'

'No.'

'Never mind. I'll buy my own. Don't laugh at me, Kit. I can help you. You've no idea of the pleasures in store. You know Anna, don't you? Anna Masters, a perfectly delicious child. I've had her weeping on my shoulder since you've been away. Positively weeping. If only you wouldn't pretend to be such a Puritan . . .'

Kit looked round him with interested revulsion. In this world old women drank themselves to death, politicians sold themselves, fat poets delighted in becoming panders. Through it all he seemed to see his father walking complacently blindfold: Kit wanted to strip the bandage off his eyes, he wanted to make him look. It was his father's duty, he suddenly felt, to find out about Porcher and Seton and Mrs Monument, and, not least, to find out about Kit. But the man was indifferent, he would not be enlightened; with complete selfishness, he had gone away for the weekend.

'You're lucky, Kit. Only once in my life have I had anything like her. Listen. It was Autumn in Chelsea and I'd had a macabre fancy to visit the Pre-Raphaelites in the Tate . . .'

Kit put an unlighted cigarette into his mouth and gazed at Seton. 'Go on talking,' he said. 'You're making me sick.'

'Why,' Sylvia was asking, 'is it that I feel so peculiar? Have we eaten too much?'

'It's Sunday,' Kennet said. 'I always feel like that on Sunday. I wake up feeling all right, the sun's usually shining and the breakfast's sometimes good. But then they start tolling those bells and I can't help it, even at my age, I feel as if I'd had an enormous lunch and was just beginning to dread being taken to church again.'

Sylvia stretched out her arms and laughed. 'Is that why we looked at all those churches today?'

'Oh, you might as well give in to it,' he said. For he had walked her, during the morning, down the silent landscape of city streets, had shown her the ravens in the Tower and the wide, swollen river, and sought out the perfect spires and cupolas, the stone coats of arms and urbane, shadowy doorways of the churches of Wren and Gibbs, churches in which the alderman's prayers and the endless Carolean sermons still, like light and shadow, seemed to linger. They had emerged at Aldgate where the Jews, released by their faith from the observance of Sunday, packed the narrow streets selling clothes and gramophone records and pungent, fabulously expensive food. Kennet had stood, large and smiling, among the strutting, twittering collection of salesmen, while a woman held out a bale of cloth, a man cut a transparent slice of sausage and gave it to Sylvia to taste and Kennet, with a certain awkwardness, had bought her a pair of stockings.

'It was a good day, anyway,' Sylvia said.

They had dined in the restaurant where they had spent their first evening together. The restaurant was almost empty, the waiter was yawning as they paid the bill. When they got up from the table Sylvia asked, 'Back to the hotel?'

'Yes.'

'More walking?'

'Do you mind?'

'If it's not very far.' She put her arm through his as they came out into the street. On the corner a group of shadowy young men in clean collars and neat blue suits were waiting for something sensational to happen.

'I wonder if it's sensible,' she said. 'Our staying at a London hotel, I mean?'

'I shouldn't think so. I'm too old to care.'

She started again, 'I mean, aren't you afraid —?'

'No.' Then he felt he had been too rough with her and asked, 'You won't regret this weekend?'

'Why should I? Will you?'

'Good God, no.' In fact he would collect it like his clients collected paintings or securities, a lifetime of acquisitions to leave in their wills. Kennet had collected the moments in his life, but they would be of little value to his heirs. They were moments when existence became sharp and positive enough to justify the laborious process of living, the long insignificance of death. 'It's one of the best times I shall remember,' he said. Perhaps, he thought to himself, the last.

'Really?' Sylvia laughed. 'What were the other times?'

'Going back to the beginning?'

'Yes.'

'Well,' he pushed his hands into his pockets, 'there have only been five or six. Not a wonderful record, is it, for all these years?'

'What were they?'

'Oh, just ordinary things. The first time I galloped a horse on the edge of the sea, one day in the war when we found an Italian village that hadn't changed since the Middle Ages, the first time I went to Paris as a young man. A boxing match I once won.'

'No women?'

He didn't tell her, but asked, 'And is it like that for you?'

'No,' she said. 'I'm much more stupid. I enjoy most times, but this time more than others.'

They crossed the blazing main streets of the West End and into the narrow lane behind Piccadilly where their hotel was so carefully hidden that only the most regular habitués could find it. Outside the tube station there was a flower-seller and he bought some carnations, although the hotel bedroom was already filled with the flowers he had bought that morning. He was behaving with the stupid reckless-ness of his age, which is more carefree than the recklessness of youth because it has, both in years and illusions, so much less to lose. Indeed he brought to this typical incident in the life of a young man an experience and appreciation which enlarged and enriched it. For him this evening was like one of those fabulous Continental balls which are still occasion-ally given, and which crowd the news of war and murder temporarily out of the papers, and in which even the most cynical find a mysterious satisfaction. Such occasions are not only enjoyed for their own sakes, but for the memories of a warmer and more gracious age which they evoke, and the older dancers, recollecting the parties and splendours of their youth, say, with a kind of pride, 'This is the last time we shall be able to put on a show like this.' For Kennet, Sylvia was not only an experience in herself, the last, glori-ously inappropriate pleasure to be celebrated in the austere years of his middle age, but she was the memory of all the other women he had known, for whom he had bought flowers and who had thanked him by holding his hand more closely.

'We've got enough flowers in that room to last a week.'

'I wish we could stay a week.'

She nodded solemnly, and then said, 'We haven't any cigarettes. You know we'll want some.'

'Of course. I remember. We must buy some.' He looked up and saw a neon sign swung at the entrance to an alley. 'They might have some here.'

'But it's a club,' she protested, following him down the stairs. 'Do you belong to it?'

'I think so. I once went to a play here and they roped us in. Embarrassing sort of play.'

The bar was full. Kennet pushed his way towards it and, while he was waiting to be served, stared idly into the long, honey-coloured mirror behind the barman's head. It was a mirror which doubled the number of inverted bottles, cheap green and red glasses, and turned the faces of the customers from white and pink to a more attractive amber. At first the faces did not seem to Kennet like those of real people, but like a crowd painted in a mural, a realistic mural of some medieval pantomime. The man with the glistening tonsure, whose long black hair curled over his coat collar, was surely a comic, bibulous monk. Vaguely, Kennet noticed his resemblance to the poet Seton, whom he had met at his own house. And then he saw his son's face. Kit was beside Seton, looking straight at the mirror and at the reflection of his father's eyes.

There was only a small space between them, but it seemed a distance as vast as the empty, sand-covered bull-ring at the time when the preliminary skirmishes are over. Kit stood, dark and slim, facing his father, who moved slowly towards him.

'Kit.' Kennet's shoulders were hunched, his big hands at his sides. He spoke quietly, as if he and his son were alone in the room.

'I went home,' Kit said. 'I heard you were in the country for the weekend. Did you come back?'

Kennet stopped suddenly. The attack had come suddenly

from the wrong side, from the young man who always had the sword. 'Come back? I never went.'

He moved sideways and leant against the bar. As he did so, Kit saw Sylvia. He stared at the throat of her black dress which, cut low, showed the firm flesh of her breasts, the golden chain tight round her neck. He looked at her and hated her.

'You know Sylvia Urquhart of course . . .' Kennet spoke as if he were feeling tired.

'I do. She's my landlady.'

Kennet took in a breath before he spoke again. 'I've been trying to find you, Kit.'

Kit looked from his father to Sylvia, but said nothing.

'Before this . . . happened, before this weekend, I was trying to find you. Oughtn't we to talk?'

'Oh, nothing unpleasant like that.' Kit turned away, facing the bar. 'Shall I buy you a drink?'

Kennet's hand came up and felt the top of his arm as if he were feeling a wound, a small hurt which had taken him by surprise. He tried to speak again even more softly so that no one else could hear. Sylvia drifted considerably away from them, Seton moved over to the piano.

'What is it you've been doing, Kit? What have you been trying to do?'

'Shouldn't I ask you that?'

'Certainly, if you want to.'

'I don't want to. We should never have met here, that's all. Everything was going all right.'

'Are you sure of that?'

'Quite sure.' Sick and viciously angry, Kit stared at his father. He felt cheated and betrayed. The image which he had at first rejected and then, when it was almost too late, desperately tried to find, turned out to be an old man furtively engaged in deceiving his wife. He wanted to burst out into the air; escape, violently, from himself and his father, and from the events they had created. Farther up the bar Sylvia was engrossed in stowing the packets of cigarettes into her handbag, Seton was whispering to an acquaintance by the piano. The barman walked away from them, following his wet cloth up the glass surface of the counter.

'Kit, I don't know what we've drifted into. Obviously we can't talk now.'

'Obviously.'

'I believed –' Kennet rubbed the top of his arm thoughtfully, his eyes were puzzled, as if the pain were unaccountable and unexpected, 'I believed that I shouldn't interfere. That as soon as you could you should be quite free. I may have been wrong.' Kit said nothing. Kennet went on slowly, 'No doubt I've been selfish. I want to help now, if I can. I've been through the Monument accounts lately.'

Kit turned as if the horn had grazed him. He meant to finish their encounter now, if necessary brutally. 'It'll be over in a week, that business. I'm putting the money back. Do you want to know anything else?'

'Yes. You can't put it back unless I help. Perhaps not then. Come and see me tomorrow.'

'I can't come and see you. I shan't come and see you again.'

There was silence between then, a silence heavy with their own blame and guilt for each other. Kennet seemed to shake himself for a final effort. He said, 'Try and understand, Kit. It's not as simple as all that.'

'This evening seems quite simple to understand.'

Kennet turned away and gestured to Sylvia. She came along the bar and joined them.

'Ready?' Without looking at Kit, she slid her arm through Kennet's.

Kit said, 'There's nothing in the Monument business that need trouble you.'

'Kit –'

'And I'll keep quiet about tonight, of course.' He smiled, and his smile was savage with the final effort of driving in the sword. 'I won't give you away.'

Kennet released himself gently from Sylvia. She moved away. He stood by Kit frowning, searching to find if there was anything in his son's face, so like his own, that he could understand. 'Good-night,' he said. 'You always know where I can be found.'

'Do I?'

Kennet followed Sylvia to the door. As they reached it his hand circled her arm and he was swearing under his breath. 'Damn them,' he was saying. 'Damn and blast everybody young.'

Sylvia said, 'I'm sorry. That was a bit awkward.'

Kennet did not answer. He was filled with a great, unformulated anger which made him tremble, a helpless fury against the stupidity and ignorance of the young who, savage and humourless, fought and relentlessly destroyed the old. As he went up the stairs into the street he tripped and, holding Sylvia's arm, steadied himself. She smiled at him as if nothing had happened and, seeing her smile, he was prepared, for the night, to forget all the past and everything that was bound to come tomorrow.

Seton said, 'My dear boy. You look as if you'd seen a ghost.'

Kit had put his glass down on the counter, his fingers gripped the edge of the bar. He said, 'Did you see him?'

'Your father's spirit, doomed for a certain while to walk the earth. Yes, I saw him. I also saw, lucky fellow, what he was with.'

'I can't believe . . .'

'Oh don't worry – look, my dear boy, here she is. She usually comes down here at this time – although what for I can't imagine, unless she's thirsty and wants a glass of water.'

The girl Anna had come down the steps into the bar. Behind her was a nondescript group of men, among whom was a middle-aged man in a dirty mackintosh who walked with a stick.

Kit walked towards them. When she saw him the girl looked up: she seemed neither pleased nor surprised and she said nothing. He passed her without looking at her and, when he had gone by, she only blinked a little, as if he had hit her in the face.

11

The Retreat

Next morning Kennet was dressed early and looked out of the hotel window, his empty pipe between his teeth.

The streets had a pale, bleached appearance, as if they had for a long time been sunk under deep water, which had only lately been drained away. Slowly and with detachment he turned and looked round the room, learning it by heart for future reference. He memorized the stocking over the end of the bed, the shoe on its side on the floor, the way Sylvia's hair fanned out over her pillow as she slept and the easy turn of her wrist.

He sat down on a chair at the end of the bed, his big hands folded together and the pipe between his teeth sticking upwards into the air. He felt as if he had swum a long way and was lying on a remote beach, miles from his starting point. Whatever his vanity told him he knew in his heart that he might never be able to get so far again.

The sunlight, bright but without warmth, fell on the bed, and Sylvia opened her eyes. Kennet didn't move.

She looked at him blankly at first and then stretched her arms and rubbed her eyes with the backs of her hands. Then she smiled. He thought how curious it was that the night had not increased their intimacy but had lessened it, so that they were meeting again, for the second time, as strangers.

His ideas about her, too, had been washed away, and although he thought her more beautiful than he had before he no longer knew what she was like. He wondered if her smile and greeting were sincere or affected and decided both that he had no means of telling and that it was quite unimportant.

'Hullo,' she said. 'I love you.'

'Good. Have some coffee?'

He handed her a cup of the coffee he had had brought up and she propped herself up on her elbows to drink it.

When she'd finished she put down the cup and lay back on the pillow.

'Are you worried?' she said.

'Of course not.' He put his pipe in his pocket.

'Good.'

'It's all good,' he heard himself speaking as if he was listening to an actor on a stage, hardly audible and very far away. 'It's all very good indeed.'

'Never been better?'

'No,' he heard himself assure her. 'Never been better at all.'

He kissed her and she put her naked arms round him, over the broad shoulders covered in heavy cloth, and her warm hands held his neck.

After he'd left her he paid the bill and walked out into the street. He bought a cigar from the tobacconist in the corner and smoked it as he walked to his office. As he went the feeling remained with him, he was still like a man who has been on a long voyage of exploration and returns to his everyday life with a new detachment, a man who, having discovered and named a new mountain range, can no longer feel the same obsessed interest in his assessment for income tax.

When he got into his office he found his letters sorted on his desk. The letter from Rolley Monument was on top of the pile. He had read it several times before his managing clerk arrived and came in for his instructions.

'Harrison,' he said, 'bring me the Monument box will you. And find me a train. I've got to go down there this afternoon.'

It was possible to feel detached, he reflected, but not for long after nine o'clock in the morning.

Kit woke late and sat up on a horse-hair sofa. His coat and trousers were folded with great neatness on a chair, although he had no recollection of having taken them off. His shoes were side by side under the chair. The whole thing looked like the arrangement of clothes in a convict's cell or in the dormitory of a backward preparatory school.

His mouth was dry and the side of his face ached. He put his hand to it and felt it to see if it was swollen and, when he touched his jaw, it felt like a hot rubber ball. He looked round the room slowly and critically, drawing no conclusions.

It was a hideous room, although its ugliness made no impression on Kit. The wallpaper was coffee coloured with an inevitably recurring pattern of pagodas. The paint work was chocolate and, apart from the sofa on which he had apparently slept, there were two cane chairs with bursting cushions and a table with a green baize cloth. On the mantelpiece there was a pipe rack and a silver tankard marked with some inscription. Over the mantelpiece there was a line engraving representing an obscure moment in an eighteenth-century naval engagement.

Kit got up and put on his clothes. As he stood up he felt worse. The side of his face ached and his head throbbed steadily. He found half a broken cigarette in his coat pocket and lit it. Then he ran his fingers through his hair.

There was a telephone on the table and he pulled up an upright chair and went and sat in front of it, looking at it. There was a lot to do; principally he had to ring up Katz. That was quite easy, he only had to pick up the telephone and dial a number he knew. Somehow he didn't do it. He was tired and uncertain. He no longer knew what he wanted.

The door opened and a man came in from the bedroom. He was a short, hard man with a face the colour of old newspaper and a clipped, grey moustache. His hair was wiry and half grey and half brown; it grew close to his head. He had pale grey eyes and his hands were long and very thin. He wore a sweater and a pair of ancient grey flannel trousers and walked with a stick.

'Hullo,' he said. 'I'm sorry I had to sock you.' He pulled his lips back and gave a grin. The process seemed to lower, rather than raise the temperature, as if he had opened a window on a cold morning.

Kit said, 'So am I. Why did you?'

The man limped energetically to the sofa and sat down, one leg stuck straight out in front of him. He disregarded the question.

'Noakes's my name. You're welcome to stay here as long as you like.'

'Then I won't be here to lunch.' The words came to Kit but he didn't say them. He looked at the man on the sofa without expression. He still felt too tired to move. He was thinking, for the first time in his life, that what happened now was not up to him, he could sit quietly and listen and find out what it was going to be.

'I had to sock you, you see,' Noakes said, 'because you socked me first. Look here, you came out of that club so damned angry about something, and you thought I was in your way, so you let out. Then I just had to cool you off and bring you home. No hard feelings?'

Kit said, 'I don't see why there shouldn't be.'

'Look here, old chap, have a mug of ale.' Noakes scrambled to his feet and found a screw-top bottle in a corner cupboard. He poured a little of it into a glass and gave it to Kit, taking none for himself.

'I suppose you're thinking I'm a rum sort of cove.'

'I'm not thinking about you.'

'What upset you so much in there anyway?'

Noakes leant his back against the mantelpiece, prodding with the end of his stick at the toe of his shoe. 'Some . . .'

he hesitated, and then brought out the word as if it hurt him, '. . . some woman, eh?'

Kit threw the end of his cigarette at the fireplace. In his tiredness he could feel himself letting go, going soft. He no longer cared what happened and he no longer cared what he said.

'Yes. And my father.'

Noakes pursed his lips and nodded as if the answer pleased him. He got down into a cane chair and stuck his good leg over the arm.

'Look. Have you got anywhere you particularly want to go this morning? Would you like to stick here for an hour or two?'

'What d'we do?'

'I usually go to the boozer for a bite of lunch. It's not bad. We could have some beer and, well, get to know each other. Then, if you want a fight, we'll come back and have one with the gloves on.'

The man made no impression on Kit; he imagined he was being handed out some peculiar line designed for emotional delinquents or anti-social members of boys' clubs. It didn't annoy him. He was pleased and relieved that he had woken up at an unknown address where no one could find him. He felt as if he had fallen ill and come under the care of a curious and half-mad nurse who had misjudged his disease. All the same he didn't want to recover. He didn't want to get back into the world again.

Kit said, 'I don't want to fight you, I'll stay a little while.'

'Good show,' Noakes grinned again, hard and icily. 'Maybe you won't regret it. I'll go and get an old jacket on.'

While he was out of the room Kit fiddled with the telephone again. He even lifted it off its receiver and listened to the dialling tone. But he didn't dial, and when Noakes came back into the room he put the receiver down almost guiltily.

'All right, old chap. Look here, would you like some iodine for that face?'

'No. Just don't hit it again, if you can help it.'

The pub they went to for lunch was as unappetizing as Noakes's room. It was large and dark and smelt sour. Noakes avoided the barmaid and did all his talking to the landlord. They sat at a marble topped table and had steak pie and glasses of beer. Noakes ate hungrily, grinning between mouthfuls. Kit was silent and hardly ate at all. Noakes was obviously trying hard through the meal, like someone trying to talk an alcoholic out of having another drink. His voice became more staccato, his face greyer with the effort he was making, his grin became more frequent and more bleak. Only once he broke off to stare at a lorry driver in shirt sleeves who had come in to have a drink. As he stared his eyes became lost and expressionless.

Watching his efforts Kit felt an extraordinary freedom and release. The dark pub, the unlikely meal, the fanatical face opposite him seemed so dream-like that the facts of life, the old woman who had died, the young woman with his father, his implication with Katz and Porcher, also became unreal and remote. When they went back to Noakes's room its emptiness, its vacuity and loneliness welcomed him. He again felt safe and he realized that when they had been out in the streets he had been frightened.

'Play chess?' Noakes was still working hard.

'Thank you. I think I'll sleep a little while.'

'Good idea,' Noakes seemed relieved. 'Look here, there's a routine I go through in my bedroom most afternoons. P.T. you know. Of course I can't knees bend but I do swing a set of Indian clubs, so if you'll excuse me.'

'You go ahead.'

Kit lay down on the sofa and for a while he listened to the tight breathing of the man exercising himself in the next room. He smoked a cigarette through; but he didn't look at the telephone.

★

Sylvia tried to telephone Kennet that afternoon but found he had gone to Worsfold. The house was empty but the boredom contented her. She changed her clothes very slowly, looking at herself all the time in a long mirror. Then she went down to the basement.

The lodgers were all out and there was no one in the house. No one in the street outside. It was a fine day of the sort which, by its uniform, unvarying brightness can be more alarming, if you are alone in a house, than the more comforting fog. Moreover there were noises in the house, clicks of doors which opened although there was no wind and banged again suddenly, sounds which could only have been footsteps on the staircase. Sylvia was not frightened but the weekend had excited her, left her exposed, as if she had lost a skin, to the smaller sensations of the afternoon.

She tried to read but could find nothing to hold her attention. She wished her child was home again, and would have been glad of the sound of Urquhart's typewriter in the room above. She wanted someone to call, and yet she dreaded seeing anyone. Finally she went to the mirror on the dresser in the kitchen and, pulling back her hair, submitted her face, eyes, eyebrows, teeth and gums to a long and exhaustive scrutiny.

She was listening all the time to little, hardly audible sounds and when the door bell rang, it seemed to shake the house like an explosion. She started and put down the mirror. Then she walked slowly up the stairs to the hall. There was a shadow against the glass of the door and she stopped and looked at it. The house was quiet now and there was no other sound when the door bell rang furiously again. She ran the rest of the way down the hall as if to stop the ringing and pulled the door open. She saw a thin man with his finger on the bell, and one eye that had no expression. When he saw her Katz took his finger off the bell.

'Kit Kennet live here?'

'Yes.'

'Is he at home?'

'No.'

'Did he tell you to say that?'

'Why on earth . . .'

She was outraged, as a child at being doubted.

'All right,' he pushed past her into the hall. 'I'll see for myself. Which is his room?'

She took him up the stairs without speaking and showed him the empty room. Coming down he walked behind her, so quietly that she might almost have forgotten he was there, until the bottom of the stairs when she felt his fingers close round her arm and he twisted her round towards him.

'Where is he?'

'I don't know.'

He seemed to notice suddenly how hard he was gripping and withdrew his hand; it was trembling as he put it in his coat pocket. His voice, which had risen, became quiet and ingratiating.

'I want to see him, lady, that's all. Important business. Tell him I called.'

'Who are you?' Sylvia moved back from him, rubbing her arm.

'He'll know. Tell him I called, lady, and he'll know. Only I'm bound to find him, see? Important business and nothing's to go wrong with it. Not while I'm around anyway, nothing's got to go wrong. Just tell him, will you?'

He was smiling now and had become almost cheerful. Sylvia nodded without speaking.

'You can tell him I mean this business to go through, see. Tell him it's going through.'

'I'll tell him.' She would have said anything if she had thought it would make him go.

'That's all right, lady, I'll go now.'

He went to the step and turned round:

'Just don't let him try anything funny, not him or any of you. It mightn't be healthy.'

She watched him go out of the gate and down the road

and then she shut the front door and put the chain on it. She went down to the basement and put the wireless on as loudly as she could and sat on the table to smoke a cigarette. She didn't understand what had happened, she didn't want to think about it. She wanted her child.

12

Family Affairs

Sandra Hume's sadness was gentle and yet sharp, like a mild attack of influenza. It was thus that partings, even with the most trivial acquaintances, affected her. If someone she had hardly known left the village, and she felt they would never meet again, her eyes blurred, her stomach felt empty, her limbs ached. It was a sensation she did not dislike, and she had felt it again, only slightly intensified, after Mrs Monument had been committed, haltingly by the vicar, stumblingly by the local market gardeners who carried the coffin, to the wet, yellow earth of Worsfold. The accustomed Anglican prayers, the sight of the children looking so clean and behaving so well, concealed for her the ultimate brutality of the occasion, her emotions, limited and sincere, were sufficient but not overwhelming.

The family conference afterwards had taken place in Mrs Monument's house. Kennet had spoken to them all and had read them a will. Sandra had not seen behind what he said, any more than she had heard the cry of despair behind the thin voice of the vicar reading the burial service. When Kennet had left to catch his train for London she had also felt sad at his departure, this big, tired man, who had seemed to her to have dealt with the occasion so well. It was she who had seen him off, the other members of the family remaining strangely silent and aloof. When she had closed the front door she wandered back into Mrs Monument's drawing room where the family were still sitting.

She took their silence as part of her own sadness and sat

down reverently among it, as if she were still in church. And then, also as if she were in church, a vague boredom overcame her and she looked about her, noticing the pretty and well disposed objects that her aunt had collected, wondering what would happen to the Bristol glass and Chelsea pottery, knowing that Rolley would claim the largest and most ostentatious pieces, but hoping, in all her sadness, that something at least would come to her.

Sandra sat at the end of the sofa, keeping as quiet as possible, hardly breathing, anxious to join in the reverent gloom she thought she saw on the faces of her relatives. Her pale fingers strayed along the arm of the sofa and toyed with the lid of an inlaid work table. She saw the shiny, walnut lid, patterned in darker wood, and imagined the neat rows of cotton reels, the armoury of pins and needles, the skeins of bright silk and wool that would be marshalled in it. Idly, with nothing better to do, she lifted the lid and peeped inside. There were no cotton reels and no skeins of wool; only, against the cushioned interior, there lay a new bottle of gin with the seal unbroken.

She dropped the lid and from that moment the scene seemed to drift, before her eyes, out of the somnolence of respectful mourning into a nightmare she didn't understand. The faces no longer expressed conventional sorrow but bitterness and distrust. Major Hume, short as a dwarf in his favourite chair, had an inhuman distaste painted on his features. Vernon was slumped in an attitude which was almost a caricature of sullen discontent. Sandra's own sister, sitting in the chair opposite, looked older, her face was lined and hard and her mouth turned down at the corners. Rolley was standing in front of the empty grate, his fists sunk in his trousers pockets.

Rolley said, 'He as good as admitted there was something wrong.'

Sandra started as he spoke. She felt horrified and embarrassed as if, an hour before, one of the bearers had fallen and dropped the coffin.

Major Hume put the tips of his fingers together and peered over them.

'It's unsatisfactory. Very unsatisfactory.'

Vernon Hume said, 'We should never have trusted her with those Kennets. She couldn't be trusted.'

Sandra looked quickly from one to the other of them. She couldn't understand what they were saying and felt as if they were all utterly strange to her. The room was cold and she was frightened.

'Someone's going to pay, someone's going to answer for it.' Rolley spoke between his teeth.

'I certainly think we should have advice.' Major Hume's hands came together and he went through a washing motion; in the quiet room Sandra could hear the sound of his dry skin.

'Advice be damned. I'm going to the police.'

'No.' To her surprise Sandra heard her own voice. She had a vision of great boots advancing over the freshly turned earth in the churchyard, of blunt fingers searching the house, opening the work table beside her. Before she could say any more Vernon turned on her.

'Keep quiet, Sandra. You don't understand anything about it.'

Her sister looked at her coldly, as if from a great distance away.

'Leave it to Rolley,' she said. 'He's right, something's got to be done.'

Sandra looked from one to the other of them, there was no comfort, no sadness left, only the signs of a struggle which she did not understand, and which she felt had left her utterly alone.

'There's no black queen so I use a threepenny bit.'

Noakes found the threepenny bit and put it on the chess board, to which it gave an undignified and untidy appearance. Kit nodded and moved a pawn in a conventional opening.

'Still angry?' Noakes asked when they had played a little while in silence.

'With you?'

'No. With your father. You were saying something about your father.'

This Noakes, Kit thought, was like a town in which you spend an hour waiting for a connection. A bleak uncomfortable town, with no public park in which to sit, and no chance of even getting a decent meal: the only thing to be said for the place is that it marks a stage in the journey, it is an advance, by so many miles, on what has gone before.

'No. I'd forgotten him.'

Noakes nodded. He seemed less anxious to talk than before. In the evening light he was even more grey and colourless, as if he might fade into the background of the dingy room. With long, slightly bent fingers, he took a piece that Kit had left unprotected.

'Treats you badly, does he?'

'He couldn't treat anyone badly.' Kit felt as if he was talking to himself, putting things into words for the first time in his life. 'I'm not sure if he could treat anyone well. His idea, he always says, is just to live.'

Noakes thought it over, twisting the knight he had taken between his fingers.

'And what does he mean, do you suppose by that?'

'Jumping into bed with stray women, apparently.' When he had said it Kit felt better. Yet it wasn't what he had meant to say, what he had meant to say was that it was the rejection of good and evil which appalled him, the reduction of all heroism and all crime to the level of commonsense.

'Is he old?'

'More than old, he's out of date.' But Kit decided not to talk any more and concentrated on the chess board, disentangling himself, in the silence that followed, from a dangerous position. Even as a chess player there were limitations to Noakes. And then, as Noakes thought out a move, Kit thought of what he had said. If his father's life, the taking of the days as they came to you, the correct behaviour in face of their inevitable triviality, the sudden grasp of pleasure, if that was not enough, then what was there, what, in the end, was going to prove satisfactory? Not the excitement of exercising power over Katz and Porcher, that was all past, put behind him by the blank wall of Mrs Monument's death: looking back it seemed as unsatisfactory as his father's life of a man of moderate sensuality. Katz and Porcher could look after themselves, he'd got past them now, he had no longer any need, or impulse, to telephone them, to set things in action.

He looked at the grey man opposite him. For all his eagerness and incisiveness, the austerity of his life and appearance, the way he exercised and trained himself as if every day were spent under the eye of an implacable authority sorting out potential officer-material, Noakes had no idea of the next move. He gazed at the chess board as if it were a crevasse and he had forgotten how to cross. And yet, since he had stayed with Noakes, Kit felt hopeful, as he had never done before, that by the time he came to leave the grey monotonous room, and the man whom he would never see again, he would know, almost with certainty, how he wanted to spend his life.

He leant back in his chair. Outside the window the street was lit with a low spring sunlight, children were squatting on the doorsteps. Inside the room became more like a cave, a hermitage sealed by dusty lace curtains from the sunshine and the street. Looking out Kit felt no nostalgia and no regret. For the first time since his journey to Worsfold, he smiled.

Noakes made some sort of a move, sketchy, inapposite. He said, 'What's going to become of him, your father, I mean?'

Kit stopped smiling. 'He'll go on,' he said. 'Just the same as ever. Nothing'll happen to him. Nothing ever does.'

★

The fat man said to the girl, 'Still waiting?'

Anna steadily finished her cup of coffee.

'No,' she said. 'Of course not.'

This time Seton didn't attempt to sit down beside her. He shifted from one leg to the other like a delinquent butler trying to apologize, while still not quite sober, for having smashed the crockery.

'I can't think how it happened.'

'Why worry?' Anna still didn't look at him.

'And when he went off with that curious character he hit . . . Who was he, by the way?'

'I don't know. I'd never seen him before.'

'Monstrous. I tell you, Anna, I'm confused, so confused. I'd made quite certain you'd be a success together. I'd gone to trouble, a lot of trouble, arranging it for you.'

'Shut up now, will you?'

'It's only . . . What can you make of people nowadays? Hunger, thirst, sex, nothing seems to mean anything any more. What can you go on? That's what I ask myself. Anyway, Anna, dear, what are you going to do now?'

'I've got a job.' She put her cup neatly back in the saucer.

'Fascinating. What is it?'

'Assistant to a dentist.' She pronounced the title carefully, with some pride.

'Ludicrous job.' Seton smiled absently. 'But in all this there seems, somehow, no necessity for poetry. No necessity at all.'

He looked at her frowning but she made no comment, and he abandoned the problem, shrugging his shoulders and walking uncertainly, like a man in a dark room, towards the door, his hands held out in front of him. When he got outside he pulled on his little cap again, turned up his coat collar. He would go home, and still in his overcoat, scribble a poem on the backs of the envelopes in his pockets. The poem might be false, incomprehensible, fashionable, facetious or, by some accident, beautiful and true. Anna would not be interested in it, neither would Kit. They were as far from him and remote, he felt, as scientists who explore the stratosphere or the ocean bed whilst he, in ridiculous beach clothes, botanized among the rock pools, delighted with his small discoveries and about, always, to be cut off by the tide.

As the days passed, Kennet began to feel, like Kit, that time was suspended, that the past had been suddenly, quite abruptly discontinued, and that when he started moving again it would be towards a different, and entirely unexpected, destination. On most days the sun shone, and he often walked the whole way from his house to his office, his hat gripped behind his back, his eyes wrinkled against the light. He didn't ring up Sylvia, being half afraid of a change in her when they met again, being half reluctant to take the further step towards her which would now be necessary. The incident, which he suspected of being the last he would enjoy, was too good, he felt, to spoil, and he disliked the thought of their inevitable discoveries and disillusionment, the slow lessening of surprise in their encounters, which time would bring. He was too old to feel a duty to drive their relationship farther, to force it to the conclusion at which it must disintegrate and die. He was too old to feel it necessary to exploit and experiment on a love affair, until, like a sinking patient, it dies under the knife. He was old enough to wait.

Everything, he thought almost luxuriously, as he loitered down the pavement, observing the progress of the magnolia in the park, could be left as it was. He had arrived, surely, at a time when neither hunger nor anxiety, ambition nor despair, goad a man farther. He could walk, as slowly as he liked, and note the trees, the buildings, the young girls, things other people would enjoy after he was dead. What compensations he had he could preserve in his own way. Time had done with him. He was no longer on the move.

In fact he was wrong. Even as he walked past the new

grass, which would soon be cut for the first time, he got nearer his office. Every morning's walk began another day, up the broken stone staircase, his hat on the front of his head now, and his hands in his pockets. He still regularly entered his room, sat down in front of his desk, swung his chair experimentally, grunted and filled his pipe. Then he lifted the telephone and sent for his managing clerk.

One morning Harrison came in looking worried, as if there had been a nasty leak in the upstairs lavatory.

'A man's got into the front room, sir,' he said, 'who says he's from the police.'

Kennet paused, his pipe half-way to his mouth. He swung his chair round and looked out of the window. Naturally, he thought, there would be a man. Time was never suspended, it whirled them all, him and Harrison and Sylvia and the plane trees in Lincoln's Inn Fields, remorselessly, purposelessly, towards a nameless destination.

'Shall I say you're busy, sir?' Harrison prompted.

'No, I'm not busy. No. You show him in.'

By the time the visitor arrived Kennet was facing the door, and his pipe was smoking steadily.

13

Question Time

Inspector Pound was surprised by Kennet. He had inter-
viewed solicitors in smart Mayfair offices, or in back rooms
in the East End, but this one, somehow, didn't look the
type. His stomach hurt him and he was embarrassed.

'Would you like anything,' Kennet said. 'A pipe of
tobacco. A cigarette?'

Cool customer too. Pound leant forward, his hands
spread on his thighs, his belly hanging uncomfortably
between them. His eyes were dull with too much good
fellowship at too many reunion dinners. For Pound there
were two sorts of people, the comical, pitiful little crooks
he hounded without mercy and about whom he had a store
of jokes, and the good chaps, the Oddfellows, the boys on
the square. Sometimes, it had been known, the boys on the
square became crooks and then it brought tears of bewilder-
ment to the always moist eyes of Inspector Pound.

'I tried to find you, sir,' he decided to start off respectfully, 'over the weekend. Might I ask where you were?'

'You might,' said Kennet. 'But I shouldn't tell you.' And
then, observing his visitor critically, he went on, 'I know
what you'd like. You'd like a cup of tea.'

Kennet himself never drank tea but he knew they had it
incessantly in his outer office. He rang for a cup which the
Inspector drank gratefully, holding the saucer carefully to
catch the drops. As he drank, Kennet watched him, almost
with affection, perhaps, he thought, the condemned man
looks as affectionately at his executioner, whose arrival he

has long awaited, and thinks, 'poor chap, he's got a nasty job.'

'Tell me, Mr Kennet,' the Inspector put his cup down slowly on the desk, 'is your son a partner in this firm?'

'No,' Kennet spoke slowly. 'My son occasionally takes messages to a client or does routine work for me. He has no partnership and no responsibility.'

'The information I had was a little different.'

'Then your information was wrong. All questions of a client's investments, trusteeship, testamentary dispositions, are entirely my responsibility.'

'Mrs Monument, I take it then, was a client of yours?'

'A personal client.'

'Your son had nothing to do with the conduct of her affairs.'

'Nothing at all. I believe he had met her socially, but that was all he knew.'

'You advised her on her investments?'

'I advised her on everything.'

'You have the accounts connected with her property?'

'I have. I can produce them when necessary.'

'Will you produce them to me now?'

'No.'

There was silence. Kennet was not damning Kit any more. He felt no resentment at the decision and responsibility he had to take, he took it naturally and did not question that it was himself and not Kit who must take all the consequences. If it was to end now, this careful life which he had, after all, enjoyed then it must end. There was no help for it. Kit had a future to think of and he, well, he had had, at least, some sort of past.

'Will you have another cup of tea, Inspector?'

'No. You know, of course, of Mrs Monument's death.'

'Her death?' Kennet stopped filling his pipe, his voice was very quiet. 'Yes, of course.'

'She died in a motor car accident, didn't she?'

'I believe so.'

Kennet had not until then, stopped to think fully of Mrs Monument's death, and now its unfairness struck him. It seemed wrong, suddenly, that Hester Hume-Monument, an arrogant, kind, shrewd, wayward, eccentric woman out of his own time, devoured by her love for a son of Kit's generation should be dead before him. Kennet had liked her as well as he had liked any woman he had not loved, she had made people laugh at her and she had not been afraid of anything, least of all of appearing foolish in the eyes of the world. She had been a good woman, and a generous one and now she was dead.

'It appears,' the Inspector said, 'she drank.'

'Yes. She drank: she missed her son.'

'There may have been a reason for it I dare say,' Inspector Pound conceded. 'I'm not saying there wasn't at all. All I'm saying is we have received certain information about certain transactions of property during the period before her death . . .'

'From her family?' Kennet suggested.

'Mr Kennet, you know us well enough, sir, to know we never divulge the source of information. I'm warning you, sir, that if these inquiries go on we shall have to obtain a great deal more information from you.'

'You'll have to get power to obtain it.'

'We shall do that, you know, sir.'

They would. Kennet knew.

'Very well. Then we shall meet again.'

'We shall meet again.'

Pound rose awkwardly. He seemed to have an appeal to make which caused him some embarrassment.

'Mr Kennet . . .'

'Yes, Inspector?'

'In these cases there's often a partner, or a clerk, someone in the office or connected with it who takes too much on himself . . . or goes off the rails . . .'

Kennet was silent, giving him no encouragement.

'The gentleman in your position often hasn't got time to

go into all the details and things are done without his notice, so to speak.'

'That doesn't happen here,' Kennet said. 'Everything that's done here is my own doing, and Mrs Monument, Inspector, was my very own client.'

'In that case I can only say good-day then, for the present.'

Pound stood up slowly, his mouth had hardened. It was as if a desperate attempt to get a man to join the Oddfellows had failed, now they were enemies. Kennet put out his hand but he didn't take it.

'A man in your position,' he said, 'isn't wise to keep things back from the police. He has a long way to drop.'

'From where I stand,' Kennet told him, 'I can see the whole way down.'

With that they parted.

When he had gone Kennet telephoned his wife.

'Hullo,' he said. 'Can I see you?'

'Today? What on earth for?'

'For lunch, apart from anything else.'

'Is it important?'

'Yes.'

'I suppose so then.'

He arranged to meet his wife at the Ritz, ensuring, by the desirability of the setting, that she would keep the appointment. On his way to lunch he called in at his club and found the secretary in a quiet corner of the smoking room.

'Richards,' he said, 'I want to resign from this club.'

'My dear chap, I'm sorry. Aren't they treating you properly? . . .'

'Perfectly well, thank you.'

'I know some of the new members are a little bit beastly, but we have to keep up the numbers . . .'

'The new members are delightful. I just can't afford it any longer, that's all. I shall have to resign as from today.'

'Kennet. We could perhaps do something.'

'It's no good. I'm very hard up.'

'Perhaps I could recommend you a few rich old lady clients . . .'

'That's very funny,' said Kennet. 'So will you take me off the list?'

'If you insist.'

'I do.'

He came into the Ritz bar and found his wife already seated at a table. One thing to be said about her, he thought, was that she was never late, he was always punctual himself and hated waiting, although he had waited many hours for women in his life. She was wearing a black suit and smoked a cigarette as she read a book she had got from the library on her way up. Kennet saw the title on the dust cover, it was called *Sexual Behaviour Patterns in Maori Civilization*. As he sat down she shut the book.

'Hullo,' he said. 'How are the Maoris?'

'Don't be absurd. You didn't ask me here to discuss books. Now what's the matter?'

'Trouble.'

'Not Kit?'

'No. Just something in the office. It'd take too long to explain. Two Martinis, please.'

The drinks came and he paid for them with a grimace.

She said, 'Explain.'

'Would you divorce me?'

It hadn't meant to start like that. He didn't know how he had meant to start, or how much he had meant to tell her. He was sick of the conversation before it had begun and only wanted to end it; he felt more uncomfortable, more in danger, than he had felt at any time during his talk with the police.

'Divorce you? Because of another woman?'

'Possibly.'

'I don't think so. Why should I?'

He sighed and felt along the edge of the table.

'I've made some mistakes at work. They might turn out

badly. Possibly very badly. Anything might come of it. Someone might prosecute, I don't think it's likely but there's a remote chance.'

She looked at him with her eyebrows raised, her lips parted and she breathed out, 'You fool.' He went on, disregarding her:

'If things start looking bad it might be better, for you and Kit, if we were divorced. The money due to you under my will I'll put in any trusts you like to mention. The income won't be large but you should be able to live on it, either in England or anywhere else you choose. There's no need to make any great decision for a week or two, but the time may soon come when you won't want to be tied up to me. I thought I should warn you.'

She was still looking at him.

'Have you been . . . dishonest?'

'You could call it that.'

'How filthy.'

He lit a cigarette and finished his drink, smiling.

'You might go away and stay with someone for a week or two. Kitty'd be glad to see you, I should think, or Charles, or you might go to a hotel. I'd have liked you to take Kit with you, but he's so damned elusive, I can't find him.'

'You said Kit wasn't mixed up in this?'

'He isn't.'

She took a cigarette and he lit it for her.

'Really, Christopher,' her voice came out on a sharp sigh like a pebble blown across ice. 'When I married you I knew you were stupid, unimaginative, dull. I knew you had no interests outside your law, and your ideas had never got farther than the Victorian age. I knew I'd have to rely on myself and my own friends for any intelligent sort of existence. I didn't bargain,' she whispered, concealing the unusual sentence from the respectable drinkers around them, 'on having married a crook.'

Kennet stabbed out his cigarette. The joints of his fingers were white.

After a silence she said, 'Did you think of Kit when you got involved in this?'

'Yes,' he said. 'As a matter of fact I did.'

'Very well,' she said. 'If this trouble, as you call it, comes, I'll divorce you.'

'And not unless?' He wanted to know where he was.

'Of course not. When will you know . . . how bad it is, I mean?'

'In a day or two, I should think. I'll tell you.'

They said nothing. With complete detachment he watched her take out a handkerchief and wipe her eyes, and yet he knew that somewhere, at the heart of her, was a deep well of unhappiness for which he should have had respect.

He said, 'I'm sorry . . .'

'You're sorry. What do you imagine all the people we know are going to say?'

'Well,' he took out another cigarette and struck a match on the table-stand. 'I don't know many people nowadays and your friends are very enlightened and progressive. I should have thought they rather admired the anti-social, criminal type.'

'Don't you realize,' she said, and for the first time there was a note of hysteria in her quietened voice, 'Don't you realize how they'll laugh?'

That was about it. They'd laugh. As far as he was concerned they could laugh themselves sick.

'I'm sorry,' he said again. 'Perhaps if my mother'd fed me properly or my father hadn't believed in God, or we'd just never married all this would never have happened. As it is I'm trying to make the best arrangement I can to keep you out of it. I can't expect you to be grateful.'

'No,' she said. 'You can't.'

They went in to eat together and managed to keep up appearances like two successful, middle-aged people who have nothing in the world in common, except the memory of the long cold war which has been the story of their married life, and which has reached the state in which no peace offer, however desperate or sincere, is ever regarded without suspicion and contempt, but in which both realize that neither side still have the courage, or the strength, or the stupidity, to join battle in earnest.

14

Afternoon

'This is it.' Katz swung off a high stool by the telephone in his Paddington garage which served for a warehouse, factory and office, and spoke to his wife, a tall rubbery woman, with hair like yellow sponge, who loved Katz. 'Tonight. Five o'clock all these dates can go off.' He jerked his thumb towards the rows of girls in sweaters and high-heeled, ankle-strapped shoes, who were busily making small plastic umbrellas to pin in the lapel. 'We'll get the place cleared up.'

'Who was it then?' she asked.

'Archbishop of York. Now I've got to make some contacts.' He was grinning and seemed excited. His wife stood by him anxiously as he telephoned and then, as he listened to the telephone ringing in an empty house, hit the rest, tried again, and again got no reply, she put a hand on his arm. He shook her off.

'Get off my back, will you?'

Katz dialled again, jabbing the dial with his finger as if he hated it.

'If this Kennet's run out on me . . . I . . . Hullo. Kit Kennet? . . . No, I'll ring again. No message.'

He hung up carefully.

'I'm not being stopped on this. I'll finish anyone who tries to stop me on this.'

He spoke quietly, through his teeth. His wife went to the desk behind them, found a packet of cigarettes and gave him one. She lit Katz's cigarette because Katz's hands were trembling.

'Do you need him so much?' she asked. 'This Kit, whoever he is.'

He frowned and then drew deep on the cigarette.

'I'll get him,' he said. 'I'll get him this evening. I've got the contact and I'll get Lord Bloody Porcher. I want this over with. Now get lost this evening somewhere.'

She left him slowly, regretfully, as he went back to the telephone. She always wanted things to go right for him. She wanted people to do what he told them, for her husband's sake and their own. When people didn't do what Katz expected, she got frightened, as she was frightened now.

On her way out she caught a girl slipping a dozen brooches into a handbag. She sacked the girl quickly, before she should get hurt.

Porcher had the club library to himself. He was sitting in a padded arm chair after lunch, reading a book of Western romances. On the glossy cover a gun spurted, the bullet nicked the wrist of the outlaw before he could draw. Porcher read furtively, knowing that he ought to be back in his office, unable to resist the dreamlike world of adventure in which he felt he ought to have existed. Life was simple then, no one expected you to talk economics or understand statistics, you had no social duties towards foreign ambassadors. The speech which Porcher had made with such rousing success to an audience of working class radicals twenty-five years before, and which he had been making with only slight variations ever since, would sound fresh and new if made from the steps of the saloon in a gold rush town.

Porcher shifted uneasily in his chair; in spite of the Western the real world kept breaking in, the world and the plan in which he was recklessly, inextricably involved. The aim of the plan was money and at the thought of it, of any large sum of money, Porcher shifted on his buttocks with embarrassment. He saw himself giving it to his wife, who would be terrified of it, would buy a new, unwanted hat and a washing machine which would fill her with terror and would then file the rest away, sick with apprehension, in a suitcase under the bed. Or Porcher himself could carry the money around, bulging in his note case, at nine o'clock in the West End, trying not to meet a reporter. The bitter thing about the whole situation, to Porcher, was that he had got into it by trying to be kind, by trying to help the people who wanted the stuff, trying to show that men in power are still human. The irresistible urge to say, 'That's all right, old boy. Leave it to me, it can be arranged,' had been the downfall of Porcher. There was nothing so very wrong in it, after all, he told himself, unconvinced. The stuff was Government surplus, the Government would most likely dump it anyway – why shouldn't the people who wanted it have it?

He had almost convinced himself that he was a public benefactor, helping trade, when a page called his name and he started as if he had been shot. When the boy came up to him he put his book in his pocket, put an indigestion tablet on his tongue and went down to the telephone box where a call was waiting for him. He shut the glass door carefully, picked up the receiver as if it was going to explode, and whispered into it.

Sylvia Urquhart, when she had given her child its lunch, washed her hair. She stood in the big, rather cold bathroom, by the bath with its great claw feet and brown stains under the taps, with her shirt off, naked to the waist. Her head was against the soft white light from the window and her hair fell forward in a brown plume. The back of her neck, slim and rarely exposed, was revealed and looked surprised. She pulled the towel across the back of her head, and her scalp tingled. She thought about nothing at all.

Gradually, however, as the rough towelling warmed her head, memory returned. She pushed the hair back from her face and rubbed the steam off the bathroom mirror and looked at herself. Then she smiled. She thought of Kennet as a past holiday spent in the hot sun. It was as if her body were still a little burnt and aching. It had all been wonderful, but it was unlikely she would be able to afford to go again. And now she was back at home a lethargy overcame her, she would have been glad to have seen Kennet if he came, she could not bring herself to telephone him: if he did not come it would, perhaps, all be just as well. Although she had welcomed the pleasure he brought her she was not hungry for it, a very little satisfied her and she was contented, on the whole, as she was. She enjoyed, as much as anything, washing her hair and looking at herself in her bathroom mirror. People of Sylvia's sort, although they might enjoy the experience if it were forced upon them, see no need to put themselves out to fly the Atlantic or visit Rome, and consequently, through indifference, cannot face the initial difficulties of getting a passport or buying tickets. So, when she was dressed, she took herself, beautiful as she was, back to the basement. On her way through the hall she met her husband.

'Going out?'

'Yes. Something's happened. I've begun my book.'

'Then why not stay in?' she gestured helplessly, 'and get on with it?'

But he was gone and the front door shut. She looked after him almost with regret.

In his flat the poet Seton also looked at himself in the mirror. He had finished lunch and made tea and this was the hour, if he had not given up writing long ago, for composition. As he saw his big, expressionless face in the mirror the words crashed in his head like displaced ship's furniture during a storm at sea. He had no wish, no power, to organize them. Instead he frowned at himself and pointed a thick index finger into the air; what rôle he was playing only he could say, he might have been a mock serious clown, or a fat public prosecutor at a political trial. The door bell rang and he shuffled to it, opening it on the eager Urquhart who was carrying a sheaf of papers.

'It's you, damn you.' Seton spoke cheerfully. 'Why don't you stay at home with your wife?'

'Something important's happened.' Urquhart pushed his way in. 'The first chapter.'

'Oh, have some tea then. You haven't written it?'

'Well, not actually, I've started and I've made notes. Let me tell you . . .'

'Why don't you tell your wife?' Seton sighed. 'That, I always imagined, was what writers' wives are for.'

'I tell you. She wouldn't understand. Sylvia's completely extroverted and my book has an entirely subjective plan. It starts off . . .'

'Don't tell me. Let me guess.' Seton wandered to the gas stove, bringing the pot carefully to the kettle, Urquhart followed close behind him, sniffing like a dog. 'It starts off at your prep. school. You're the dirtiest, most unattractive little boy there and desperately in love with the head-master.'

'You're quite wrong.' Urquhart sat triumphantly down on the table. 'I'm in my first term at my public school, of course I am rather unpopular. There's a very interesting relationship that develops between me and . . .'

'Oh well,' said Seton. 'We might as well talk. I've got to stay in this afternoon in any case. I'll explain to you that the reason that I no longer write is not that I'm tired of writing, but of writers. As I said to Parson Dobson, with whom we discussed vocations last night over a bottle of wine, my vocation is to be a small town, provincial undertaker, defer-ential and rich, full of elaborate phrases in bad taste in praise of the departed.'

'The book ends,' Urquhart went on hopefully, 'with my adolescence.'

'Good. A book should always end somewhere.' Seton poured out the tea and gave himself too much sugar. 'Or else an auctioneer, a violent little auctioneer selling up the accumulated treasures of generations of mad old ladies . . .'

'If you had time,' Urquhart said, 'to listen, I might read you just the first paragraph . . .'

'Of course I've no time to listen.' Seton perched himself on the edge of the table. 'No one's got time to listen, only to talk. I tell you,' he held the cup and saucer up to his mouth, his lips sucked in tea, 'I tell you people are like a collection of the deaf and the blind, shouting accounts of their own nightmares into a high wind. When we discuss vices they say Seton's vice is egoism. Untrue. You're a hopeless egoist, Urquhart, picking away at your utterly ordinary childhood; forgetting that the only faintly significant thing about you is that you have a wife and child. And your wife's an egoist and as for Kit Kennet and Anna Masters, my young friends, they are the supreme capital I's. I suppose old Kennet, tied up in pink tape among his deed boxes, is an egoist as well. But I'm not, Urquhart, I'm not. I look at you all and sink myself into the background like a bird watcher in a tree. It puzzles me, sometimes, why I do it.'

'Yes,' said Urquhart. 'Very true. Now I wrote this bit because it was a particularly vivid experience which I have never forgotten.'

'Oh God.' Seton put down his cup on the table. 'Forget it now, then. Try hard to forget it now.'

But Urquhart, making himself comfortable in the corner, had already started to read. With a sigh Seton took up his cup again and listened, resigned, at last, to his lot.

Noakes came up to Kit as he stood and looked out of the window.

'Nice weather.'

'Yes.' Kit flicked a cigarette end into the street. Then he turned away.

'Tomorrow,' Noakes suggested, 'we might take a run out into the country.'

'Thanks. I'm going tomorrow.'

Kit lifted and carefully replaced the beer mug on the mantelpiece. Noakes leant against the window sill, his hands in his pockets, his tweed coat pulled up over the flat seat of his trousers, ready for the quiet talk with the leaving boy, the manly hints about the world outside, the invitation to next year's reunion dinner.

'I shan't ask you where you're going.'

'Good.'

'I'm sure we'll soon meet again.'

'I'm sure we won't.'

'Oh, come now . . .'

Kit turned and sat on the sofa, he looked comfortable and assured.

'Why should we? All the same, thank you. You've been a great help.'

'That's all right, old man.' Noakes stared at the toe of his shoe. 'I've been glad to do what I could. I've helped a good many chaps down at the club and elsewhere, who've been a bit in the dark.'

Kit said. 'I'll beat you at chess. Stop talking nonsense.'

Noakes smiled, half ashamed as if he had been caught out in some indecency. He sat down by Kit who was setting up the board.

'You may laugh, old scout, but I'm sure I've shown more people than most how to get the best out of themselves.

'No, you haven't.' Kit's face was almost savage. 'No one can do that for anyone else. No one at all.'

As soon as he said it he was sorry. He was sorry for Noakes who would be swinging his Indian clubs in a fumed oak bedroom in the days to come, days which stretched out for Kit in an interminable, glittering, variegated sequence, linked by a pattern he could, at the moment, hardly comprehend. Tomorrow, perhaps, he would begin to find it out.

Mrs Kennet sat forward in the chair eagerly, like a young

child or an old woman. The light from the window searched her face with the ruthlessness of a cross-examining counsel. Dr MacAndrew was by no means ruthless; he lay back in his office chair, blurred and shadowy against the light, and tiredly brushed the dandruff off the shoulder of his black coat. He had grey hair and bits of it were always falling out, like the hair of a badly kept dog. His legs, in crumpled sponge-bag trousers, were stretched out in front of him and he seemed almost asleep.

'You know how we've never got on,' Mrs Kennet was saying, 'and now he's suggested a clean break. I suppose it would give me a new scope, release me and leave me free to give what I can to Kit. Do you think so? Do you mind my asking?'

'If the relationship has become useless,' MacAndrew intoned like a worn-out gramophone record, 'divorce is often the best way out.'

'Years ago I thought we might come to some sort of terms, but now it seems impossible. He seems to put up a wall, a barrier of insensitiveness and stupidity to all up-to-date ideas. I feel helpless with him, maddened sometimes.'

'At his age men,' MacAndrew spoke as if he had discovered a profound truth, 'get into a rut.'

'And now, apparently, he's gone and got himself into this squalid mess.'

'And when they're in ruts,' MacAndrew blew his nose loudly on a rather dirty handkerchief, 'they try and break out, once for the last time. A sort of last fling as it were. They assault typists in trains or cut off schoolgirls' hair.' He spoke sadly of their activities, without relish. 'Anything to try and prove they're still young. Something driven underneath,' he put away his handkerchief and got to work on his fingernails with a penknife, 'comes boiling to the top.'

'It's nothing like that.' Mrs Kennet sank back in her chair, shielded her eyes with her hand from the light. 'Nothing to do with sex, I mean. He's got into some mess over money.'

'Money's only symbolical.' He bared his yellow teeth for a moment in what seemed intended for a knowing smile. 'Only symbolical of something deeper, more emotional. We know that, don't we?' It was the phrase he used to those who seemed reluctant to pay their bills on the way out.

'The point is,' Mrs Kennet pulled a glove tightly up her hand, letting the rings stand up like warts on the black skin, 'if we cut off from him now, Kit and myself I mean, will it leave us with any guilt, any feelings we shan't be able to resolve, any tension if you can understand me? I wanted your advice.'

MacAndrew's chin sank into his collar. He appeared to be thinking.

'He's a sick man, Mrs Kennet, a sick man. You know that. Will he come and see me?'

'You won't get him here alive.'

He finished with the penknife and put it back in his pocket. 'We can't help,' he said, 'those that don't help themselves.'

'He's so stubborn,' she said. 'Do you know I honestly don't think he realizes that there's anything wrong with him.'

'Ah, that's the trouble.' MacAndrew pulled himself up in his chair, coming moderately to life. 'They don't realize there's anything wrong with them, they bottle it up, force it down, and then it gets too strong for them. Then it breaks out and we get these sad, sad businesses, like your husband over this girl in the train.'

'Not a girl. Money.' Mrs Kennet corrected him absently, still pulling at her glove.

'Ah yes, money.' He had lost interest in the conversation again and hauled a big metal watch out of his waistcoat pocket. 'We must go into this, go into it deeply. Next time. Naturally you're worried about your own daughter.'

'We haven't a daughter. Only a son.'

MacAndrew stood up, looked silent and knowing, as if he felt it was safer that way. When he stood, his trousers and waistcoat were rucked up and it was revealed that he was wearing boots.

'Fix a time with my secretary for next week,' he said. 'Then we'll go into it really deeply. You'll find a cheque form,' he added, 'on her desk.'

Mrs Kennet emerged into the sun in Wigmore Street and blinked. The eagerness, the youthfulness and the age had left her. She was again timeless and efficient as she walked into the Times Book Club to change her book; she gave instructions as coldly as she might eventually give instructions to a solicitor to petition for a divorce. The talk with MacAndrew had given her something she apparently needed and, by an act of faith, she was able to feel she had wasted neither her time nor her money. She accepted him, this unattractive, forgetful Scotsman, as a bulwark against the loneliness which she was too intelligent to fail to see before her, but which, for reasons he could never explain to her, she was helpless to prevent.

When Kennet came back to his office after lunch he saw Harrison, his managing clerk, drying his handkerchief in front of the coal fire in the outer room. There was nothing superficially attractive about Harrison, he had two strands of dark hair which he dragged across a bald head, he had a bad cold and a duodenal ulcer and the sleeves of his vest showed under his shirt cuffs. At the same time Kennet felt a sudden rush of affection for this man who had been in the firm longer than he had, who did his work punctually and efficiently and showed not the slightest interest in the private lives of the clients for whom he was responsible. He would have liked to have found out more about Harrison, now that the time for doing so was possibly short. He knew that he lived with a widowed sister in Wimbledon, an address to which Kennet carefully sent a bottle of port and sherry every Christmas, as his father had done before him. It occurred to him that he and his father might have been quite wrong about Harrison's drinking habits and that the house in Wimbledon was crammed to the doors with undrunk port and unappreciated sherry. Instead of asking Harrison about this, however, he walked into his inner office.

Methodically he began to tidy his desk, an operation he normally had little time for. He filled a wastepaper basket and straightened the pencils in their tray. He felt curiously lighthearted, as if for the first time in his life he was in sight of some sort of freedom. He sat down and opened a drawer and found a packet of tobacco which he opened and made into a mound on his desk. He was smiling as he filled his pipe, and still smiling as he pushed the rest of the tobacco into his pouch, brushing up the grains with the side of his hand.

Had this not happened, he thought, he would have died at this desk, married to the woman he had married before time had changed every cell in her body and frozen every impulse of her spirit, automatically carrying out the duties he had imposed upon himself. As it was he had a new career, raffish, unburdened, free. He would trouble no one and no one would trouble him; from his moderate, middle-class position of power he would abdicate, anyone could have it who wanted it, he was free. If he chose he could sit in the sun, work with his hands and let his mind sleep, let die in himself the last vestiges of his father's joyless and painstaking religion of work. He pushed down the tobacco with a broad thumb and carefully lit his pipe. Except for Sylvia he had no regrets.

Sylvia, he knew, however, would forget him. She must forget him for, in the future, he would be of no use to her, he would be a liability, an object of pity, to everyone he had previously known. As he had no intention, in the future, of feeling sorry for himself he didn't mean that anyone else should feel sorry for him. When he went away he would go alone.

Characteristically he hardly thought, as he contemplated his future, of Kit who had caused it all. He would do this for Kit as he had given him his schooling, sheltered him, clothed him, as he would have paid his debts. After it Kit could do as he pleased. Perhaps, and the irony of the thought pleased him, Kit would come through it with his reputation unscathed, make a sensible marriage and recover the family business. That would be all right. He wished him joy of it. Perhaps Kit's way would continue solitary so that they might meet, at some distant future, disclassed, dispossessed, as equals. He would have liked, had he been allowed to, to know his son. He thought, with regret, that had he not known himself and his limitations so well he might have succeeded in knowing Kit better. He had been content, perhaps, to admit that the generation which opposed him baffled him, and, when the chance of resignation came, he almost welcomed it.

The pipe was smoking well and he finished it, sitting forward in his chair, his hands knotted, his eyes almost closed. When the pipe was finished he knocked it out in the ash tray, blew down it and put it back into his pocket. Then he lifted his desk telephone.

'Harrison,' he said. 'Get me through to Scotland Yard, will you? Inspector Pound.'

'Yes sir. There's a lady here to see you, sir. She says it's important.'

'Oh.' Hell, he thought, can't he tell her I've done with clients. 'Who is she, Harrison?'

'A Mrs Hume, sir. A Mrs Vernon Hume.'

The wife of the man with the codfish eyes who had started it all off, come, like her husband, full of righteous indignation. All right, he could stand it.

'Show her in then.' he said. 'I'll make that call later.'

15
Sandra

That afternoon Sandra had sat in the greenish marmoreal recesses of a church behind Sloane Square and gripped a silver and white order of service in her hand. On it she saw, for the last time, the name that had thrilled her whenever it appeared on a list on the school notice board: 'Olive Hunter-Rampton', soon to be transformed and simplified into Olive Sproult. Beside her sat a middle-aged woman in lavender tweeds whose neck was already flushing the colour of Tudor brickwork, as the organ panted into a preparatory anthem.

'Friend of the bride's?' This woman whispered in a fatherly way to Sandra, who was looking young and almost pretty as she craned to see the altar.

'Rather!' Sandra hissed back enthusiastically. Between two black straw hats she caught sight of Captain Sproult, nervous and pale, in the uniform of the Grenadier Guards, awaiting his destiny in the shape of Olive, former head of Sandra's dormitory and, in the general view, the decentest girl in the school.

'Friend of the bride's, too?' Sandra hissed back.

'I was her moral tutor,' the woman breathed confidentially, and, as if discussing some private female disease, she flushed more deeply, 'at Oxford, you know. Were you up with her?'

'No.' The family funds had never run to Oxford. 'I say, most of us here seem to be friends of the bride's.'

'I was just thinking as I came in, the bridegroom hardly

seems to have any friends at all. Still, friendship doesn't seem to mean nearly so much to men, does it?'

'I suppose not . . . Ssh.' The organ had worked itself into its preliminary triumphant chords, a draught from the open church door hit Sandra on the back of the neck, behind her she heard a rustling of silk. She contorted herself, trying to peep round without staring rudely, and there saw Olive, in a few minutes to be Sproult, Hunter-Rampton as was, as her mother's friends would say when they tried to identify her, tried to decide, from among her numerous cousins, which she was and which children she had had. Now she came cleaving up the aisle, without her glasses, the lack of which gave her face a screwed up, questing expression, big boned, healthy, eager and ready for matrimony, garlanded for the sacrifice, bearing on her arm the desiccated Hunter-Rampton, a small, weightless man, dried and withered by the Indian sun, tormented by asthma, who was amazed at the urgent womanhood of this daughter who, it seemed to him only yesterday, he had left with an aunt in Wokingham as a complacent child of ten.

For a moment Sandra felt a slight disappointment. Olive's marriage had been late, she was older than Sandra and yet Sandra had been married during the war and Nicholas was five. Lately their letters had dropped off and they had not met for some years; a disloyal suspicion crossed Sandra's mind that Olive's late marriage might have been due less to her own quest for perfection than to reluctance on the part of the eligible men. She had not remembered that Olive's eyebrows joined quite so thickly over the bridge of her nose. Doubts were, however, allayed as Sandra sank in prayer, suddenly conscious that she had laddered her stocking on her way down to the hassock. As the bridesmaids passed, with the pages in kilts and the little girls carrying posies, and as the moral tutor beside her started to cry, she was filled with emotion. Marriage, she suddenly knew, was a glorious, a blessed thing, it affected her like children and puppies and happy endings in the cinema and brought a lump to her throat. She forgot Vernon and felt that she would like to be married again, to anyone who would ask her. The muttered responses thrilled her and she clasped her hands together. When she slid back to a sitting position she had forgotten the run in her stocking. She wanted to be kind to everyone.

It was during the vicar's endless, inaudible colloquy, and intimate, and confidential, talk on marriage which Olive, now Sproult, and her groom the Captain, stood stolidly and took as if it was a scolding from their father; it was while this buzzing was going on at the end of the church that Sandra thought of Kit. She thought, inconsequently, of his hand on the arm of his chair that morning at Aunt Hester's, and the atmosphere in the church was such that she felt a longing to protect him. She knew something of what had gone on in the family since her Aunt Hester's death. She had observed it and she had reserved her judgement. She stood up and sang a hymn, she sang out in a thin, rather flat, touching voice that was a little hoarse from cigarette smoke and a cold caught at Worsfold. The moral tutor beside her opened her mouth to keep up appearances, but did not sing. Now, Sandra thought as her spirits rose with the singing, she was free, free until her train left Paddington. Vernon was hunting and the children were at Peggy's. If she wanted to stop Rolley having things all his own way, then she knew she could.

At heart Sandra was romantic, romantic in a hopeless, untidy way, without either real energy or conviction. She was moved, still, by endless Victorian novels, by the sky over the hills round Worsfold and by the celebrations of the church. She was devoted to her children, not with the savagery of a vixen possessing her young, as was her sister Peggy, but with a detached pleasure in childhood itself. She had an urge to do good which the life in Worsfold, with its concentration on the battle against overdrafts and the slaughter of animals, did little to satisfy. Moreover her imagination had been captured by Kit.

So her plan came to her as she stood singing, a thing she only did furtively at the pantomime at Christmas and, with slightly more confidence, in church at her friends' weddings. It matured afterwards at the reception when, with a glass of champagne in her hand, she stood next to Olive and felt a return of unquestioning devotion. The two women leant towards each other, almost shouting over the hysterical clatter of relatives' greetings.

'Nicholas is a darling. Of course Vernon can't see it, but he's awfully good looking. You must come and stay.'

'Love to . . . Have a piece of cake, Nanny.'

'How are you, Miss Sandra? I haven't seen you since you used to come and stay and climb trees . . .'

'Oh, I'm married now, Nanny.'

'Really! And wasn't Miss Olive a lovely bride?'

'Such a nice sermon, what you could hear of it.'

Sandra drank some more champagne, bringing back memories of an endless summer afternoon with herself up an apple tree reading *Jane Eyre*. Over the hat of Olive's devoted nurse, she caught sight of the brick-red face of her cousin Rolley, joking with Captain Sproult. She knew Rolley had come up to the stag party, but she hadn't seen him in church; his presence seemed to her to add a note of coarseness, almost of fear, to the occasion. She drifted away into the crowd, still holding her glass. Her plan had become a determination.

As she moved towards the door, the moral tutor looked up before her.

'I've spoken to her,' she said, in the tone of one who has seen Naples and is about to die. 'And now I must run. Can you remember at all where one put her coat?'

'I'm just going too,' Sandra said. 'I'll help you find it.'

But, the moment she could, she excused herself and found a telephone box. She lit a cigarette to steady her nerves and then found 'Kennet, C.' in the book. She took a taxi in Knightsbridge, and, quarter of an hour later, drove into Lincoln's Inn with her heart in her mouth and her handkerchief, wrapped into a small, hot ball, clutched in her hand.

She had keyed herself, as she was shown into the inner office, for the sight of Kit, young, expressionless, playing with his cigarette lighter. A moment of panic overtook her, and a fear that her efforts to help him might be laughed at or suspected. She was steeled for the pain she experienced when she went to help her own child, when it had fallen over and it shouted and struck out at her. But, instead of a sullen young man, the face that looked up at her was old. The man seemed to fill the whole of the back of the desk, and at first he seemed so little inclined to talk to her that she wanted to leave quietly before their conversation began.

'I thought . . . I expected,' she began breathlessly.

'My son?'

'Well, yes.'

'Everyone seems to nowadays. Won't you sit down? I think your husband called on me some time ago.'

'Yes, he did. I think there's something all wrong about Aunt Hester and . . .'

'Yes. I know your family do. They are having the matter investigated by the police. Everything will be disclosed in due course. I am sure you'll be content to leave things to your husband and the police.'

He looked at the eager, pale young woman without resentment, rather as the bull looks round at the preliminary dart with which he is wounded before the kill.

'You mustn't jump to conclusions,' he went on. 'I'm sure you'll find that the investigation will be thorough.'

Poor child, he was thinking, she looks as if she had a permanent cold in the head. He would like to have comforted her, warmed her: even the pearls round her neck were like opaque drops of ice. He was sorry for her as he was now for all respectable people; she would still be trying to pay the baker and make the children look presentable in ten years' time when he might be sitting on an upturned barrel in San Domingo regarding, through one eye, his latest coffee-coloured child. The absurd luxury of this thought made him smile, and he saw that his smile frightened her. She twisted her handkerchief and said:

'Have the police said anything about Aunt Hester?'

'Her money? Yes.'

'No, not her money. Her . . .'

'Yes. Go on,' he encouraged her, puzzled.

'Her death.'

They looked at each other in silence. Sandra sitting forward in her chair, her mouth a little open, as if she had said something obscene, mentioned a subject like cancer or childbirth which was, to her, taboo. Kennet looked back at her thoughtfully. The pleasure which he had been contemplating, the fantasies of escape with which he had indulged himself, faded. It was as if a dream had taken a twist into reality and he had woken up. He pushed his cigarette box towards her.

'Yes. Tell me if you want to.'

'I think . . . I have been thinking, that you ought to know.'

He lit her a cigarette and she pulled on it nervously, smoking with little gasps and often tapping off the ash with her finger. He was unmoving, and, suddenly, felt cold.

'You know it happened after Kit left,' she began. He relaxed slightly. 'We were all at tea, at least I was at tea with Rolley and Peggy. Peggy's my sister, and Nicholas was behaving very badly, I'm not telling you properly.'

'Go on.'

'I think I'd better start again . . .' Kennet listened carefully, as if he were trying to pick up a clue, although her voice seemed to come to him from a long way off. He heard the story of Gerry, whom he had once met, and his mistress with her house on the outskirts of the village and his unheroic end. He heard the account of the unpleasant tea party on the day Mrs Monument had died. He listened frowning, without recognition.

168

'I don't understand what you make of it all,' he said. 'Kit was away, you say.'

'Yes. Kit had gone, but don't you see – Rolley.'

'Rolley?'

She had finished three-quarters of her cigarette and ground the rest, pink with lipstick, down into his ash tray. 'Rolley killed her,' she said calmly.

'Why did you come here?' he asked.

She blinked, as if the question was unexpected.

'I liked your son. I was sorry for him. I knew that they would try and get him into trouble. I wanted the truth about Rolley to be known by someone.'

'And you don't like Rolley?'

'No.'

It was more convincing than if she had said she hated him, more convincing, and more alarming.

'But it isn't the truth, you know,' Kennet stretched tentatively, the first movement that he had made since she began her story. 'I don't think you should say it again, or even think it.'

'It is the truth.'

She spoke with the determination of a woman who had been married without passion and, from the emptiness of her heart, had learned to detest the men who surrounded her.

'Come now. Perhaps it was tactless of him to tell her the truth about Gerry, it may even have been cruel. But how was he to know she'd drive out and see the woman?'

'I think he told her to. I think that, after he'd told her the story, he suggested it.'

'Even if he did, he was nowhere near when the car crashed. He couldn't have had anything to do with that.'

'He fixed the car.'

'That's absurd.'

'But he did fix it. Everyone knows it.'

'It was Gerry's car, wasn't it?'

'Originally it was Gerry's car. No one used it at all after

Gerry died. Then Kit, your son, had it out and took Aunt Hester in it once or twice, there was nothing wrong with it then. After Kit went, Rolley wanted to show Aunt Hester that he was a much better mechanic than Kit and he had the car down all one Sunday, said he'd completely overhauled it. She never used it again until the day she died.'

'That's all?' Kennet asked, after a pause.

'That's all.'

'Then you had better forget it. No one would even bring a charge on that evidence. Besides, you know this is your own brother-in-law. You've got your sister to think of.'

'Peggy's got nothing to thank him for. Neither have I.'

Kennet saw tears in her eyes, tears as cold as the pearls round her neck. He looked uncomfortably out of the window; but at her next words he looked back at her, smiling.

'Forgive me,' she was saying. 'It's very stupid; but I've just been to a wedding.'

'They always affect me like that too,' he said. 'It was nice of you to want to help Kit.'

'I did want to,' she said. 'Funny, because he rather frightened me, and I don't suppose he liked me. I only thought, if he could be left alone for about ten years, well, something might come of him, if you know what I mean. Something different from Rolley, anyway.'

'It's a possibility.' Kennet hesitated, then he said, 'I expect your brother-in-law's still out at Worsfold.'

'Oh no. I saw him this afternoon. At the wedding as a matter of fact. Peggy told me he would be staying tonight as well.'

'Do you know where he stays?'

'I think the Motorists' Club.'

'Oh yes, the Motorists'.'

They sat in silence while she looked at him appealingly, her energy suddenly spent, wondering if she had done wrong. Before her stretched the cold train journey, the sullen husband in the draughty house, the child she hardly understood her only compensation. Her fingers began to twist.

'Don't worry,' he said. 'And try and forget what you said.'

'But have I helped at all?'

'Oh yes, helped. Of course. It was nice of you to come.'

When she had gone he sat still for a while longer, then he got up and shook himself, as if shaking off the last remnant of his fantasy. He got his hat off the back of the door and went out slowly, regretfully. In the outer office Harrison was, once again, blowing his nose.

'Good-night, Harrison,' he said. 'I'll be at the Motorists' Club in half an hour if there's a message.'

'Yes, sir. And Scotland Yard?'

'They can wait.'

16

Conversation in a Club

The 'Motorists'' was not far from Kennet's own club, although its world was different. You could swim, play squash, and dance occasionally at the 'Motorists'', the members often brought ladies in to dine there and the *Auto-car* was the magazine most in demand in the library. Enquiring of the hall porter, Kennet learned that Rolley had just left the club, but a friendly member, a tall character in a blazer with gold buttons, who glowered over an enormous moustache with an air of lunatic helpfulness, told Kennet where to find him.

'The "Archery" in Wardour Street. Rolley Hume went there for a drink. Wanted me to join him but I was tied up with a bloke. Up from the country, Hume, trying to make the best of things.' The member's laughter became uncontrolled, like the revving of an engine when the accelerator slips, and Kennet left him and walked across Piccadilly and up Shaftesbury Avenue. His steps, which had been hesitant as he left his office, grew firmer as he walked. However, he was feeling no pleasure. If what he meant to do succeeded he wouldn't, he knew, be particularly triumphant. With an effort, a final heroic effort for which he felt altogether too old, he might just succeed in putting things back as they were. The thought added no elation to his walk.

At the 'Archery', when he found it by the neon target and arrows hanging over the door, they investigated him through a square glass hole before he was admitted. A doleful Scotsman took his hat, and he paid him half a year's subscription for the pleasure of coming to talk to Rolley. Rolley, he learnt, was inside.

Kennet went inside and blinked, horrified. The room seemed to him empty, and he felt as if he had walked on to the stage for some nightmare performance of a play about an English county family. This was partly because the whole room was lit with hard strip lighting which made no secret of the mahogany panelling, the tapestry chairs or the castellated concrete chimney-pieces. The light glared in the inglenook, polished the wrought-iron fire-dogs and the suits of armour and shone to special advantage on the numerous oil paintings of bibulous abbots and gourmandizing nuns. Recessed behind a triumph of halberds and pikes was a small and hideous bar, from which lowered a man whom, but for the carnation in his buttonhole, it would have been difficult to distinguish from the decapitated moose and bison which also adorned the walls. Rolley was not in the room, but there was a half-emptied drink and an open *Evening Standard* on the bar.

Kennet crossed to the bar and the attendant, whom he took to be also the manager, served him with a whisky and soda.

'You been here since we did it up, sir?'

'I've never been here before.' Kennet sipped his drink and looked round him. Rolley was still out of the room.

'We flatter ourselves we've got a real cosy feeling here now, you know. Harrods did us proud on the pictures, you've got to admit that.'

'They're very convivial.'

'You know we've tried almost every setting here, believe it or not.' The manager talked urgently, like someone in an outpost of the Empire who has not seen a white face for years. 'We tried rustic, you know, thatch over the bar sort of wheeze, and Spanish, we had Spanish shutters opening all round the walls, then we tried modern. Nothing drew the patrons like this is going to, Country House Comfort, that's what's going to put the "Archery" right back into the swim. Do you know what we're going to do here, sir?'

'No.'

'Bring back the 'twenties.'

Rolley came in then. He had changed, after the wedding, into a grey flannel suit and a soft shirt. He was still red in the face and his eyes looked dirty. He swung himself on to a bar stool beside Kennet and finished his drink. The manager refilled it automatically. Rolley looked at the back of his evening paper and then threw it down as if it had insulted him.

'When's there going to be anyone in here, George?' he asked.

'Well, that's not fair, Mr Hume. Admit there's not a crowd in tonight, but there's you and this gentleman, new member.' The manager's long, animal face waved hopefully between them.

Rolley spoke without turning to Kennet.

'Good–evening,' he said.

'Have another drink,' said Kennet. 'I've got to talk to you.'

'Thanks I will, but who the hell are you?'

'My name's Kennet. I was Mrs Monument's solicitor.'

Rolley paused with his drink on the way to his mouth. As the situation sunk in his colour deepened and he looked round angrily.

'Christ, Kennet. I've got nothing to say to you. I believe Scotland Yard have.'

'I didn't say that. I said I wanted to talk to you. Now have another drink.'

'You trying to get round me or something?'

'Perhaps.'

'Well, you won't succeed. I hate a shyster. Always have.'

The manager was gazing into the distance at the farther end of the bar waiting for someone to get hit. When Kennet called to him to fill up the glasses he made an elaborate performance of starting out of his reverie.

'Take that drink,' said Kennet, 'and come over to the other end of the room and talk.'

He picked up his glass and walked towards the farthest tapestry settee. He knew Rolley was coming behind him, coming in a mixture of righteous indignation, drink and remorse, which might, at any moment, turn dangerous. When they reached the end of the room Kennet sat down. Rolley stood, swaying a little. His fist was clenched and his lip pulled back on his teeth. As he moved he spilled some gin and vermouth out of his glass.

'You're a shyster, Kennet, that's all you are, a low, mean, dirty little shyster. That money you and your son got your claws on was meant for us. I think I'll hit you, Kennet, I think I'll hurt you.'

'Sit down,' said Kennet. 'Don't be an ass.'

The man still swayed in front of him and Kennet took out a cigarette and lit it deliberately.

'Have a cigarette?'

'Who did you pinch them from?' Rolley's fist knocked the case from his hand and strewed the cigarettes over the floor. At the other end of the room the manager, like the bison on the walls, did not blink. Kennet felt the anger rising inside him; he was not a quick-tempered man, but angry, he knew, he would lose control of the situation. As if, he told himself, it was a situation he wanted to control.

'Try not to be stupid,' Kennet said. 'If I'm prosecuted that won't get you your money back. I know I can put the money back and still be prosecuted, but putting it back depends on me.'

Rolley suddenly sat down. 'I must have that money,' he said.

'Of course you must. I give you my word it will be returned to the estate within a week. If that's done will you inform the police that you have had the figures audited and I've completely satisfied you and you don't propose to take any further action?'

'No. Damn you. Why shouldn't you get what's coming to you?'

'Do you think I'd mind?'

'Think you'd mind?' Rolley laughed. 'That's rich. I should about think you would. Respectable solicitor sentenced. Judge on gross betrayal of trust. You'd hate that. Besides I'd never heard it was comfortable in gaol.'

'I'm a good deal older than you,' Kennet said. 'At my age a respectable position has stopped being something you've worked for and started being a load on the back, a load you're quite prepared to shed. But that's not the point. What have I got to lose by a police prosecution? A few years in prison, it doesn't frighten me, the loss of my business, friends, home, you'd be surprised how I could bear it. Do you know what this seemed to me at first? A wonderful opportunity. I remember a friend of mine once coming to me with smiles all over his face and saying, "Do you know, they tell me I've got T.B., what a wonderful chance to read Gibbon." Well, that's what I felt, Hume, a wonderful chance to be all the things I'd never had the courage to be before.'

'Don't know what you're talking about,' Rolley said. 'But you're bluffing. Of course you're afraid.'

'All right.' Kennet leaned back on the settee. It was time to make the final, risky play, the gamble as to the success of which he still found himself surprisingly indifferent.

'If I am afraid,' he said, 'aren't you?'

'Afraid of what?'

'A thorough investigation,' Kennet said, 'into the way Mrs Monument died.'

Rolley looked up from his glass.

'Now,' he said, 'I know I'm going to hit you.'

'No,' said Kennet, 'you're not. You're going to keep on listening. Mrs Monument's money was no good to you when she was alive, she'd refused you an advance, even I knew that. Under her will you knew you were bound to benefit; though she might detest you all, she had a strong sense of family duty. Your mistake, of course, was letting everyone know that you'd overhauled the car – and then telling everyone you were going up to disillusion her about Gerry an hour or so before she died. Did you tell her to drive up to the woman's house, or did you just bank on her doing it?'

Rolley was holding on tightly to the stem of his glass, he was pushed back in his chair as if he was recoiling from a smash in the driving seat of a car.

'On a story like that,' he said at last, 'no jury would convict.'

'Perhaps not. But would you like to try the experiment? There'd be some anxious moments, I imagine, waiting to see whether they would or not.'

'My God, Kennet, it's a filthy suggestion to make.'

The protest, however, had lost some of its conviction. His voice was thinner and his eyes more frightened.

'All the same, I'm making it.'

'You won't get away with it. Do you hear, you won't get away with it.' Rolley's voice rose, the manager leant his elbow on the bar and started, with consuming interest, to read the evening paper. 'No one's got away with crossing me up. I never wanted any trouble, but when I get it, my God I give it back. No one's done me down and got away with it, ever since I was at school.' He stood up again and swayed over Kennet, as he got up his hand knocked his glass which broke on the floor. 'There was a bloke at the garage in Worsfold, tried to cheat me over a bill, do you know what I did, socked him. Ask anyone in the village. He never tried it on again.'

'I expect that was why you had to repair your aunt's car yourself. Can we have another drink?'

The manager looked up, startled, as if it was the first sound he heard from the other end of the room. When Kennet ordered them he brought the drinks over, smiling in a conciliatory manner between the two men. Rolley took his drink, but still stood up.

'All in all,' Kennet said when the manager had gone, 'it was probably silly of you to hit that garage man.'

'It's all bloody stupid.' Rolley grinned unconvincingly and subsided again. He had finished his drink at a gulp.

'You see, the police will probably start their inquiries with people like him in the village. It's a pity you've got an enemy, and one that knows something about cars.'

'It's all nonsense and you know it.'

'Is it?' Kennet leant forward. It was the first definite movement he had made for some time. The big, square shoulders seemed to fall forwards, bringing his grey head, his tired, experienced grey eyes into the light. His fists were clenched on his knees. 'Is it nonsense? It may be. Only one person knows that and it's you. The point is can it be made to sound sense by the police, by the witnesses they call, by a prosecuting counsel? A trial by jury isn't infallible, you know, and there have been some convictions on very thin evidence.'

Rolley was pushed back in his chair, he seemed to shrink as Kennet leant towards him.

'I'm not scared.'

'Aren't you? Not for yourself perhaps, you may be a man who's never afraid for himself, although I've had a long life and never met one. But you've got a wife, a family. How're they going to feel while they read the newspapers on your trial and wait for the verdict? How will your wife feel when she goes into the grocer's shop and everyone stops talking? Or when people in the village she's known all her life stop recognizing her? Do you think even if you were acquitted, you could still live in Worsfold?'

'Go on,' Rolley said, 'I'm breaking my heart.' He picked up the stem of the broken glass from beside his chair, it was broken off to a point, like a dagger. 'What do you think my wife means to me, what do you think I came up to London for?'

'I can guess.'

'You're a hypocrite as well as a crook, you said just now your family meant nothing to you.'

'All right, nothing means anything to us except ourselves, we begin and end with ourselves.' Kennet was leaning farther forward and Rolley held the stem of the glass so tightly that his fingers were white. 'But we begin and end with our lives. I can't imagine why, but I think you are attached to your life, that you're afraid of dying. I think you're afraid now and that's the reason, the only reason, why we shall agree about this. I'm keeping my side of the bargain and you'll keep yours, and there's no reason why you shouldn't enjoy another forty years. We shall agree about this because you're afraid, and there's no other way. You hate me but your fear is stronger than that, stronger than anything in the world. I don't see why we need talk any more.'

He got up and Rolley sat in the chair in front of him, one hand clenched on the arm, the other still turning the broken glass. Kennet felt a longing to grip the wrist, to cover his face, to prevent the attack that seemed inevitable. He turned his back, however, and walked away across the room. He knew Rolley was watching him, he thought he had not got out of his chair. As he passed the manager he saw that the man's eyes were fixed on Rolley, but he didn't turn round to share in the spectacle. He said good-night, but the manager didn't answer.

Out of the room he waited, without looking round, by the entrance of the lift. When it came, and he made sure the gates were closed behind him, he leant against the side of the lift and wiped his hands with a handkerchief. He was tired out and would have liked, other things being equal, to have gone home to bed. Other things were not equal, however. By the ash cans in the cul-de-sac at the bottom of the lift he lit a cigarette, then he found a prowling taxi and got into it.

17

The Last Encounter

Some distance from the 'Archery' but not far from Godiva
Crescent, which was the destination of Kennet's taxi, is that
area of London between the railway and the canal which is
the goal of all those who wish to lose themselves in the
anonymity of a furnished room; here is the dark triangle of
iron bridges and peeling stucco houses in which the alley
known as Maybrick Mews is hidden. To get to Maybrick
Mews you must cross to the north of the Park and penetrate
the jungle around Paddington Station, the maze of squares
and alley-ways from each of which the station, like a great
black greenhouse, is discernible in the distance. It would be
easy, if you were an innocent from the more salubrious
areas of Whitechapel or the Docks, to be misdirected, to
get lost among the second-hand clothes shops and medical
book stores of Praed Street, or to diverge into the quiet and
dignified squares round Sussex Gardens. It is between these
that the mews lie like the galleries of some dangerous and
dilapidated coal mine, dark, narrow, ridden from time to
time by inexplicable cries. In the daytime, the inhabitants
of the mews are peculiarly idle; as though at their leisure,
they wash and polish luxurious motor cars which are driven
only by night; the women come out in their bedroom slippers to quarrel with each other or with the children; the
men, exhausted, sit on doorsteps and read the backs of the
lunch time papers. At night, many of them start out about
their business, the engines of the great cars purr, muffled in
the silence. The rest withdraw and activity, noisy, violent,

concentrated, begins behind the narrow, curtained windows and locked front doors.

At the entrance to the mews, as if to guard it, there is a big, well-lit public house, and at the end of it, the darkest, most silent, most securely locked of all the buildings, is a converted garage in which were carried on the ever-changing affairs of the one-eyed man, Katz.

That evening, just before nine, Mrs Katz had gone up to the pub, having been told by her husband to make herself scarce. She was sitting at the bar with her friend, a lady dressed in a purple hat and a coat which looked like the fur of ill-conditioned Pekinese dogs. They were discussing the various internal complaints of their acquaintances and drinking gin and tonic. In the room, which smelt of stale beer and aniseed, were also two whores, a well-to-do German doctor and a ginger cat of vast proportions which sat on the bar next to the sandwiches. From a wireless in an alcove an announcer bleated some news of earth-shaking importance and the hands of the clock above the mantelpiece jerked, as though palsied, round the interminable hour.

Just after nine on the same evening, Porcher, driving his own car, stopped at the garage at the end of the Mews. When the door slid open he crossed into the garage as quickly as he could, then he waited while Katz shut and bolted the door behind him.

'By yourself?'

'Yes. Anything gone wrong?' Porcher prised the black hat off his forehead. He was sweating.

'No. Would anything be wrong?' Katz was standing under the naked light at the end of the garage, which was fitted up as an office, having a desk and chair, a safe and a calendar with a drawing of a girl in black underwear, lying on a tiger skin to answer the telephone. By the hard overhead light, Porcher saw every detail of Katz's face and the motionless eye.

'The stuff's all been indented for as surplus and for

destruction. It's out-dated small arms mostly, rifles and so on. No use to the country, of course, it's all been replaced.' Porcher sat down heavily in the chair; he looked at the calendar and then quickly away. He seemed to want to justify himself, even to Katz.

Katz asked, 'Did they send it where we told them?'

'It's in the dump at Caversham, not far from the river. As I say, as far as the record goes, it's been destroyed.'

'Good. Our contact's got a launch to pick it up from there – some friend of young Kennet's.'

Porcher put the hat back low on his forehead. The light was hurting his eyes. 'Don't tell me what you've done,' he said. 'That part of it doesn't concern me. As I say, it's all surplus material, no use to the country, you understand – hopelessly out of date.'

'The lot they sell it to won't look for the date,' Katz said. 'Probably can't read, anyway.'

Porcher held on to the edge of the desk; it was as if the room were a ship's cabin and he felt it slope suddenly. 'It's over now,' he said. 'I've done it for you.'

Katz went over to the safe and spun the combination. Porcher shifted uncomfortably on his chair; he was expecting to get paid and the idea frightened him. He patted his pockets as if wondering where he would find room for all the money. He stared at the girl on the tiger skin, his eyes small and frightened. If he could have bought her with the money he was going to get he would have found the situation equally bewildering, equally impossible to conceal from his wife. He heard the sigh as the safe door swung open. 'I'll take it now,' he said, 'then I can get away. I haven't much time, you know. I'll be glad to get on my way.'

'You'll have to wait.'

Porcher looked up slowly. There was no money in Katz's hand, but he was holding an automatic. It seemed a cumbersome weapon and he held it as if it were very heavy.

'Don't worry,' Katz laughed. 'This isn't for you. I tell

you, young Kennet's got the money. He's fixed it up with some old dame in the country who's lending it to him, although she doesn't quite know what for. He's bringing the money here. I don't think you'll have to wait long.'

Porcher looked at the gun, but did not speak. His fingers were white, holding the edge of the desk.

'There's nothing wrong, Mr Porcher. Nothing wrong at all. Kit Kennet's been a bit difficult to contact lately, that's all. When I tell him to come, he'll be here. Probably he'll come without me telling him. He'll come.'

Porcher swallowed. No sound came out of him. Katz sat down and tipped back the chair. He put the gun carefully on a sheet of paper on the desk and started to make himself a cigarette. 'I'm not out for young Kennet, you know, either. He may be playing around somewhere, but I'm not out for him.' Katz pushed the tin of tobacco and papers towards the man opposite him. Porcher shook his head, his eyes still on the gun. 'It's just that this deal happens to mean a lot to me. It's big, and I like big things. This is one of the biggest I've been in,' Katz's voice was dreamy, his fingers held his cigarette quite still. 'So I'm taking a precaution. Just a precaution in case some long nose comes poking in here. Just in case our young friend sends someone else round here, instead of having the good manners to come himself. Just in case he tries to be clever . . .' Porcher took his hand off the table. 'Don't move about too much, it makes me nervous. No one's going to stop this deal, Mr Porcher.' Katz lit his cigarette, manipulating a brass lighter with one hand. With the other he picked up the gun again. 'No one's going to live very long if they try'

Porcher tried to speak and failed. If he had shouted, he felt suddenly, Katz wouldn't have heard. Katz was distant from him, like a man entranced, his eye fixed, almost in ecstasy, on the weapon in his hand.

There was a long silence and then, at last, Katz stubbed out his cigarette and picked up the telephone.

The taxi gave Kennet a rest. He leant his head back on the cushions, breathed in the smell of rexine, as he watched the lights change from red to green along Oxford Street. In the shop windows the pale waxen women postured and held out their long fingers. The shops swung past, empty but lit up, as they would be all night, for the benefit of policemen and tarts. It was still early, the time when, normally, Kennet would be sitting down to dinner. But he wasn't hungry, he was only tired, tired as he never remembered being in his life before.

He stared out of the window and Baker Street unrolled itself, its silent, almost furtive pubs, photographers, shops for selling wigs, false busts and second-hand crockery, passed him unnoticed. They drove north of the Park, near to the house where his wife was presumably consuming a solitary dinner, past the Hanoverian gateways and irreproachable terraces to the church and churchyard of St John's Wood. There the taxi turned off into wide, dark rows of peeling houses, hidden behind dusty and uncared-for trees, until, after climbing steadily, they reached Godiva Crescent. When he had paid off the taxi, Kennet had no hesitation about the bell. Sylvia came to the door.

He was leaning against the door-post when she saw him, and she was reminded of their first meeting, when he had seemed likely to fall with exhaustion. Their greeting was, for some reason they could neither of them understand, cold, almost hostile. They were seeing each other unexpectedly, without any anticipation of pleasure, and Sylvia noticed the cigarette ash on Kennet's waistcoat, the fact that he needed to shave again at the end of the day, and a slight trembling of his right hand.

'Is Kit in?'

'He's just gone out.'

'Do you know where?'

'He didn't say.'

'Show me his room.'

She shrugged her shoulders and he knew that he was

behaving badly, lacking the time or energy to be polite. He followed her up the stairs and walked past her into the room. She stood in the doorway, silently protesting, watching him trying to find out about his son with the distaste with which she might have watched an old man searching through his wife's possessions for love letters.

It was a small bed-sitting room and was furnished like a thousand others in that part of London. No ornament, picture or piece of furniture had been altered to express Kit's personality. He had left undisturbed the Cézanne reproduction over the mantelpiece, the pot of spills by the gas fire, the basketwork chair and the hessian cushion. His only alteration had been a telephone extension installed by the bed and the only signs of his presence were a pile of newspapers on the floor in the corner of the room and the large white table lamp which his mother had given him. Kennet stood in the middle of the room, taking it in. He realized that he wanted to get this over so that he could go home for a bath and some sleep.

He looked more carefully at the room and felt himself growing cold. He knew that the girl in the doorway behind him was suddenly, for the first time, disliking him; but that wasn't what worried him. That late, unexpected love affair, like an undeserved Autumn holiday which he had taken when there was important work to do, was coming to an end. He could understand that. It was the room itself that horrified him.

Since the first night when he had sat up searching through Mrs Monument's accounts he had been looking for Kit, and since that short, bitter, almost wordless battle when he had left Kit in the crowded bar, they hadn't spoken, he had never discovered what his son felt, or knew, or had done in the affair. He had worked in the dark, trying to protect a stranger whose motives he had never understood. Up to this moment Kit had worried him, and now he was in his room, the room where his son had slept and lived and possibly made love and there was nothing, only an emptiness, a contemptuous negation which had accepted the Cézanne and added nothing of its own.

The emptiness, the lack of character, gave the room a curious terror for Kennet as he moved about it to discover, as he had to discover, where Kit was, what had happened to the money which had to be put back before Rolley's fear wore off. It was like the face of an enemy on which there was no expression, no sign of life, weakness or strength, of which he could take advantage. He looked round, frowning slightly.

'What are you going to do?'

'Look for something.'

'You can't!'

He shrugged his shoulders. Probably he had had no business to let her love him in the first place; if she had to dislike him now, it couldn't be helped.

'But why?' Sylvia asked coldly. 'Wouldn't it be better to wait? He may be back soon.'

'I've been putting it off too long already. I should have done it long ago.'

However, he seemed unhurried. He filled his pipe and lit it carefully, throwing the match at the gas fire. Then he sat down in front of the desk and stared at it. In spite of what he had said, he still hesitated. The drawer in front of him might have been locked, he didn't try it. After all, he told himself, there was really no hurry; he could wait, as he had waited all his life, believing the best of everybody, for things to sort themselves out.

Sylvia crossed to the mantelpiece and stood against it, looking down at him. She seemed to be putting herself deliberately in front of him, as if she were trying to hide something behind her back. Although he had just become reconciled to a change, the weakening and at last the death of the relationship between them, he now felt a sharp stab of desire for her, like the pain one is said to feel in the space where once one had a limb.

'I don't know what the hell to do.' He looked up at her, half smiling.

'Don't you?' Her answer was unsympathetic, disillusioned as if her feeling for him had depended on her idea of an almighty father, a man who had lived so fully that he was never at a loss.

He put his pipe in his pocket. Then he turned and looked again at the drawer of the spindly, modern desk. His hand seemed so large that it could have wrenched it open without difficulty, but he didn't move.

'When all this is over,' he said, not looking at her, 'we'll go back, I suppose, to the way we were before. Before we met, I mean. I wonder what we thought we were doing.'

'I thought you knew.' She spoke bitterly and he looked back at her, his shoulders moving under his big, loose-fitting coat in a movement of complete and patient uncertainty.

'I've never known,' he said. 'All my life I've never known. I've been content not to ask too many questions.'

'How smug you sound.'

'Only realistic.' He smiled, hesitantly. 'Only accepting the fact that whatever you ask there's no one, anywhere, to give you an answer. Except, perhaps . . .' He paused, his hand stroking the edge of the desk. 'Except yourself, if you can train yourself to be fairly honest.'

The telephone rang by Kit's bed.

It rang stridently, insistently, like a child crying mechanically for help. The sound of it made Kennet shiver; he looked at the telephone, half praying for it to stop, half wishing he were alone in the room. Sylvia looked at him with raised eyebrows. It took him all the time in the world to get up from his chair, but still the caller would not abandon hope. As Kennet moved to the telephone he felt Sylvia shrink away from him. He picked up the receiver. 'Yes?'

'Come on down here, can't you?' The voice was peremptory, expressionless. 'You're late. Porcher's been here for half an hour.'

There was a silence. Kennet didn't answer.

'What are you up to? I don't like it, Kennet. Get on your way. Do you hear?'

'Yes.' Kennet kept his mouth as far away from the instrument as he could. Sylvia said, 'You can't pretend –' He put his hand over the mouthpiece and turned to her. 'You'd better go and leave me alone.' His eyes were quite cold and he took his hand off the mouthpiece at once, as if he knew she would obey him.

'What's the matter with the bloody line? Porcher wants the pay-off now, and then he's blowing out. Get down in ten minutes. I can't afford anything to go wrong on this.'

'I'm coming,' Kennet said. 'Where are you?'

He had said too much. The silence at the other end of the line was prolonged for about a minute and during it Kennet could feel the unknown man thinking, thinking rapidly, trying to guess from Kennet's breathing how near and how strong was the ambush into which he had fallen. Then there was a click and the line went dead.

When he put the receiver back, he saw that Sylvia had gone, as he had told her to. He said, 'Porcher,' to himself, and repeated, 'Porcher.' Then he went over to the desk. It was not locked. Inside the drawer was a ruler and two pencils, both sharpened. There was nothing else.

He opened a cupboard and tried the pockets of Kit's suits. There was nothing in them. He pulled up the mattress of the bed and found nothing. He went over to the chest of drawers and found what he was looking for, a cheap notebook under a pile of handkerchiefs.

There was very little in the notebook: a couple of sheets of figures which were familiar to him from his examination of Mrs Monument's accounts, a list, and a sum of money. Kennet speculated, without deciding, what made up the list – guns that should by rights have been dumped in the Mediterranean, old army vehicles which had somehow been accounted for but still existed? They could have been either. What surprised him was that the sum of money destined, he supposed, for Porcher, was so small. He turned through the rest of the book without finding anything. On the back cover a name was written, the name 'Katz'.

He shut the book, but didn't bother to put it back, Neither did he close the gaping cupboard or tidy the bed. He took his empty pipe out of his pocket and put it between his teeth. He went back to the telephone and took a volume of the directory. It didn't seem very clever to him, but he didn't see what else he could do.

There were nearly two columns of Katzs, but he disregarded the women and the doctors, dentists and veterinary surgeons and, for some reason, those with suburban numbers, and concentrated on male Katzs with central London addresses. He worked quickly, ticking the numbers off with a pencil as he apologized for wrong numbers to a string of unrecognizable voices. As his pencil passed over the addresses he wondered at which one Porcher was waiting. If he had had time he would have felt sorry for Porcher.

After fifteen minutes he heard a receiver taken off, then a 'Yes?' he thought he recognized. Time had not improved the tone of the voice which rasped into his ear. He didn't answer. 'Who is it?' Damn you, speak!' The voice was like a pistol shot in a dark room. Kennet stayed silent. When he heard, 'Kennet . . . ?' he put down the telephone for the last time and underlined the address, 4 Maybrick Mews, tore the page out of the book and put it in his pocket. Then he went over to the desk.

He found a piece of paper and, taking out his fountain pen, wrote a letter for Kit. He told him that Rolley was frightened enough to take the money back without asking questions or worrying the police. He told him how, with the money returned, it could look all right on the books. He told him that there might be further inquiries, but he suggested how they could he handled. Then he signed the letter and folded it carefully.

It was ridiculous, he felt, to write a letter like a Will; he would probably see Kit again before the week was out. It was ridiculous, but he didn't alter what he had written. He wondered whether he should have said anything about Sylvia, or referred to their last meeting, but he had never cared to explain or excuse himself and he decided to say nothing.

He didn't know where Kit was, only guessed that he had gone away to escape from the thought of himself and Sylvia. The idea didn't amuse or anger Kennet. Like most ideas, he was prepared to accept it. He bore no ill-will, either, for the journey that he was about to make in Kit's place. He was glad that he was going alone. Throughout his life, even in the ecstasies of love, he had been strangely solitary; a kind of loneliness had become necessary to him, it was one of the reasons why he had little fear of death.

But now, as he stood in the doorway of the empty room, an unexpected, almost desperate longing for his son came over him. He needed urgently to say the things he had always, for some reason, prevented himself from saying. He felt Kit moving away from him, bewildered, into the future, and he wanted to stretch out his hand and touch him. Sooner or later, Kit would come back and read what he had written. He unfolded the letter again with the idea of adding something, but the only words he could think of sounded hollow and unreal. If anything happened, Kit would have enough to remember. If he met Kit again, he could say it himself. It was better to leave it alone.

He closed the door and went down the dark staircase and he knew that this, at least, was for the last time. He noticed a sourness, a stuffiness about the house which he had not remembered before. It was a pity, he thought, that his memories of Sylvia's house should be spoilt by this awkward, brutal search into his son's affairs, and by a smell on the stairs which he never used to notice.

In the basement, Urquhart, bending over the white paper, recalled an unkind word said to him by a school friend twenty years before. Sylvia lay on her stomach and read the evening paper. She heard the front door click as

Kennet opened it. She raised her head for a moment and then, as the door banged, she dropped it between her fists. So many people came and went in the house that her husband paid no attention to the sound.

When he got into the dark street, Kennet found that it had been raining. The pavement was wet and there was a cold smell, like the smell of steel, which he breathed in gratefully. As he walked down the street, looking for a taxi, he saw a cat sitting on top of a wall and a child staring out of a lighted window. A couple passed him, and he noticed the bright, chattering face of the girl, who had her arm stretched back to go round her young man's waist, and whose hair was still wet from the rain. It was as if these things had suddenly become more vivid to him since he had been in Kit's room, more vivid and more important, like details from a great and luminous picture. He took the pipe from his mouth, meaning to fill it, but his pouch was empty.

He found a taxi on the rank at the end of the road. When he had given the driver Katz's address, he shut himself inside and leant back, closing his eyes.

The news had finished and the wireless in the pub was playing dance music. Mrs Katz was watching the door. No one else was talking very much when the taxi stopped outside and Kennet came in to ask the barman the way to Maybrick Mews. When he had gone out, Mrs Katz finished her drink with an elegant flourish, said good-night to the company, and started down the mews behind Kennet. The click of her high heels kept pace with his footsteps on the cobbles, and she kept into the shadows by the wall. Two doors away from her home, on the opposite side, she stopped and watched.

She saw Kennet raise his hand to knock on the bolted sliding door of the garage. The door was slid open and Mrs Katz saw the big empty storage space, the single hanging electric light bulb, that was familiar to her. She also saw a fat man sitting under the light, a man in a blue suit, with a gold watch chain stretched over his waistcoat, whose weary face looked greenish under the light. When he saw Kennet the fat man laughed. He laughed too loudly, without humour, but with mingled derision and relief. His laughter was drowned by the scraping of the door as it was pushed towards Kennet. Mrs Katz saw Kennet with one hand on the door, his other fist closed. She stepped forward as Kennet got in through the narrowing doorway. Then it closed altogether. There was silence, only the narrow band of light under the door showed her that the garage was occupied.

Mrs Katz pressed back against the wall. She knew she shouldn't have been there, but she was anxious, she wanted to know that Katz was all right, and she felt safe while she watched. He would be all right, she knew, as long as the thing played itself out the way he intended. Success soothed him, calmed his nerves, made him human: if his cue made a perfect cannon, if his hand came up full of aces and his women were there when he wanted them, then Katz was easy. If he missed he could rip up the cloth, upset the table, slash a girl so that she bore the mark all her life. That was why she was anxious for Katz, anxious that things should go the way he wanted. She was frightened of what he would have to do if his luck was out that evening.

At second hand, almost telepathically, the woman understood Katz, she could understand his hysterical, frustrated violence, even when it was directed at herself. She could feel it coming now, even in the dark, even from behind the closed, dark bolted doors in front of her; just as, in the heat and darkness, she could feel the electric approach of a storm. She was frightened, not of what Katz might do, but of what the things he did would, in the end, do to Katz. She was frightened for her husband, not of the stranger shut in with him.

Patiently, unable to help, yet determined not to move, the woman waited. She could hear the traffic from Edgware Road in the distance, an occasional murmur from the trains in the station. A dog barked from another mews and, from nearer to her, a woman shouted an oath. She could hear a car being started and, outside the pub, a man began to play an accordion. A negro in a smart suit came lurching down the mews and he flashed a grin at her; she looked away proudly. When his footsteps had gone, the accordion stopped too and everything became quiet.

Ever since Katz had come back from the war, that prolonged, terrifying absence which he never talked about, things had been the same. She had looked after him as if he were sick. She felt angry with the world that didn't understand Katz, didn't understand that he would be all right if they gave him no trouble. If they gave him trouble he would hunt them and hunt himself. She had seen the gun in the safe at the garage.

It was taking so long that she became calm, the silence of the mews, now complete, was reassuring. As it continued she found a cigarette in the bottom of her handbag and lit it. It was a small, bent cigarette and it tasted of face powder. All the same she smoked with elaborate movements of her hands, and continued to watch without expression.

When the sound came she might almost have imagined it. It was a muffled explosion, so ordinary that it might have been the bolt shot back, except that the bolt was shot back immediately after. Mrs Katz started and dropped her cigarette, ground its bright end under one patent leather heel.

The door opened a little and Porcher came out. She saw him for a moment, his face dead white, fumbling for the key of his car in his waistcoat. When he found it he unlocked the small black saloon that had been standing in the mews, banged the door behind him and drove away, driving badly and too fast, almost hitting the side of the arch where the mews turned into the road. The garage door shut again.

Mrs Katz took advantage of the sound of the car to walk back towards the pub. Her face had set like a mask, but her walk was unsteady, as if she were about to fall off the high heels of her shoes.

Her drink was still unfinished on the bar. She said nothing as she climbed back on to her stool, although the barman greeted her.

Ten minutes later Katz came in. He was wearing a hat pulled down to shade his bad eye. As he leant on the bar beside her, she whispered, 'What've you done?'

'Had a bit of trouble. All right now.' He grinned at her. She hoped no one else saw the grin. It was not sane.

Katz's voice was normal, however, as he spoke to the barman.

'Beer please, Charley.'

'What've you done?' she repeated.

'I said I'll tell you later.'

'Tell me now.'

'Oh shut up, will you?' Katz's hand was steady as the beer was pushed across the wet counter towards him. 'Cheers, Charley. And how's every little thing with you, boy?'

18

And Afterwards

When Kennet died, men were dying all over London. In their beds, in rented rooms or behind screens in hospital wards, in circumstances more or less mysterious, men died in privacy and silence. Kennet died in public. Soon after his death, the newspapers turned it into a story which made him remote and incredible even to the few people who knew him. For a week his name was a household word. He might have died on a scaffold under arc lamps and his end would have been less notorious: he, who had always avoided publicity.

It lasted for a week and then the story faded. A few days after the body was found, Katz was held for questioning and then charged. A coloured man from the mews, who had heard a shot, gave evidence, and Kennet's widow identified the body. Mrs Katz, a newspaper over her face, was photographed leaving West London Police Court. Porcher, owing to an indisposition, was some days away from his Ministry and then, for reasons of health, resigned. Their figures, larger than life, flickered across the screen of public consciousness and disappeared. Kennet's death was forgotten. It became, at last, a private and credible fact, affecting the lives of only a few.

The year, at that time, turned to early summer. Typists and clerks brought their sandwiches out into Lincoln's Inn Fields and the dusty black trees outside Kennet's office came into leaf. The formalities of his death were completed; his executor, which was his Bank, dealt with his estate, negotiations were started to sell his practice. In his former club his acquaintances stopped talking about him. His death, to their minds, had something undesirably reckless about it, as though he had been caught in adultery or had issued a false prospectus. They told each other that they couldn't understand it, and discussed it no further.

When he resigned his office, Porcher also resigned from the club. The places he and Kennet had occupied at lunch were empty. In a short time they were filled by two company directors, Old Wykhamists who sang together in the Bach choir.

The consequences of an event may be limitless, but in only a little time they become weakened and remote. The ripples caused by a stone thrown into the water become, as they spread wider, almost invisible, the sparks which hang in the sky after a rocket has exploded are no more than dust. The consequence of that great event, the death of a man, may be even more ephemeral; those who loved him, like those who hated him, may have done so out of misunderstanding; his death only substitutes one false picture for another; or death may have been so long expected that when it comes it fits as naturally into the order of events as the falling of a tree which everyone has long known to be insecure. Perhaps death, like everything else, is an act of will, and a man does not die until he has lived to the extent of his own strength and his own time. In Kennet's case he had lived beyond it.

Kennet was murdered, and the circumstances were never fully explained. There were many people interested in not explaining them. So far as the community was concerned, they had what they are supposed to want, a victim. The desire which they are supposed to have, to be revenged, was not frustrated. As for the people who knew Kennet, they had their own ways of regarding the matter. But for for them, whether they loved or hated him, his death meant freedom. For the ageing man, if he has not lost all his control, is always a sort of remote, often detested

God for someone; and when Gods die, there is generally a celebration.

Inspector Pound reported to his superior officer in a room that looked out over the river and where three tulips with smuts on them, brought in by the typist, heralded the approaching summer. He was frowning, as if the inexplicable events of the last few weeks had insulted him. Crime, as he usually found it, was a thing which needed very little explanation.

'The Monument angle's dead. Nothing doing there.'

'Why not, Fred?' Both men spoke very softly, as if they were exchanging secrets in church.

'Family won't play any more. I've seen Mr Rolley Monument and he's scared of something. Anyway, he says it was all a mistake and he's quite satisfied now, so he can't see why we aren't satisfied too.'

'Are we?'

'No. But Kennet's dead now. What's the point in going on with it?'

'Ever get a look at the books?'

'No. He didn't have any partners. I suppose they'll sell the business. He may have straightened things up, of course. Without the family to give evidence, there's not much chance of a prosecution, even if we had anyone to prosecute.'

'What about the son?'

'According to Kennet, he had nothing to do with it. It was the father's show entirely.'

'Do you believe that?'

Pound shrugged. 'Maybe not. But without the family we shan't pin anything on him either. There was a bit of money moving around before the old girl died, but it's probably got back to her estate now. No, it's the other angle that's interesting me.'

'Katz?'

'We'll get a conviction all right. But he's not talking

about anything. He must be scared, but he doesn't communicate.'

'What was the tie-up there, Fred?'

'Beats me. Beats me entirely. You know I went to see Kennet some time back?'

'It's in the file. Smart, was he?'

'Not smart. I wouldn't have thought smart. Not crooked, either.' Pound rubbed his jaw thoughtfully. 'He wasn't nervous about anything, you know. More like someone who knows his number's up. Quite happy about it. Resigned, you might say, as if he knew he was going to walk into that bullet.'

'Well, we know who shot him.'

'Yes. We know that.'

'Work on it, then, Fred. Let us know when Katz says anything.'

Pound stood up. 'If he says anything,' he said.

Urquhart showed Sylvia another folder. On it was a photograph of a squat thatched cottage with windows cunningly designed to keep out the light of day.

'No main water,' he said. 'But it's only three miles from the station.'

'If you like it,' she said, 'we'll buy it.'

'Once I get into the country, I'll be able to write, I know it.'

He wouldn't she knew. He wouldn't be able to pump the water or trim the hedge or grow peas, but trying to do all these things would stop him from trying to write.

'Kennet going like that.' Urquhart sighed. 'All the publicity. It's been difficult to get work done.'

'It's always difficult. Anyway, you never met him.' She brushed her hair away from her forehead with the back of her hand. Urquhart looked at her hungrily. She had lately become mysteriously attractive to him again and he thought how beautiful she was, dressed in clothes he had never noticed before. He shut the folder. 'Can we afford that one?'

'Just about, with a little bit over.'

He had never asked her why or how she was suddenly able to buy him a cottage. He knew her father had once left her some money and perhaps he thought that she now had the use of it. If he thought anything else, he didn't ask, and Sylvia didn't tell him.

'You do want to live in the country, don't you?' he asked, rather nervously.

'If you do.'

'I mean, I can always come up for odd nights, to meet people. You can too, if you want to.'

'That'll be nice.'

'I think it's just the right sort of life for us. In Essex, everyone says, the people are much more *real* than they are in London. Anyway, you always said that children ought to be brought up in the country. Now we can do it, thanks to your father, of course.'

'Thanks to who?' Sylvia asked, and then, 'Oh, I see what you mean.' They were talking in the basement kitchen, and she walked away from him towards the mantelpiece. She picked up the china Highlander which stood at one end of it and turned the little figure over to examine its broken foot. It was here, she was thinking, that Kennet, on his first visit, stumbled, and almost fell . . .

'I thought you'd like it. It was my husband's. He was a great collector.'

The house was open and lit up, even the front door was open and the light from the hall gilded the trees on the north side of the Park. Mrs Kennet stood in front of the drawing in her husband's study, the drawing of a naked, capable girl who washed her breasts as if it were part of her day's work. There weren't a great many people in for cocktails that evening, and the few guests were disposed about the rooms so that their presence made the house seem emptier, not more crowded. The poet Seton, his head on one side, his little eyes wide with curiosity, picked his way across the carpet towards the open door of the study. He was pleased to be in the house, more pleased than ever, now the owner was out of the way. He was fascinated by the conversation that he had overheard.

'Did he have many Impressionists?' the guest, who had been shown the picture, was asking obediently.

'Only that one,' Mrs Kennet sighed. 'But as a young man, he wanted to paint, you know. I believe he might have been a great artist, but was frustrated by his work.'

Seton pursed his lips, raised his eyebrows, like a fat bandsman about to blow a dubious note on the trombone. 'Who,' he asked brightly, 'are we talking about?'

Mrs Kennet turned on him, her eyelids shaded and her black dress fitted to the throat; she wore no jewellery. She didn't answer directly, but gestured sadly, gently, towards the desk, its empty chair.

'I'm sorry,' Seton said, lowering his voice. 'I'd no idea . . .'

'No one had any idea,' she said. 'No one knew him as I did.'

She was probably taking the right line, Seton thought. She was providing an effective counterblast to the publicity she had pretended to ignore. His fingers felt for the bowl of salted almonds on the table beside him. 'Not that I didn't suspect,' he said reverently, looking back into the warm, softly lit drawing room where he always, in future, hoped to be sure of a drink, 'that he was more than an ordinary lawyer.'

Mrs Kennet, still aloof, exalted, led her guests out of Kennet's study and back to the fire. Only when the door had closed on the cold room, the large, plain desk littered with pipes, the lovely, masculine drawing, did she speak. 'His heart wasn't in his work. He might, at any time, have thrown it all up. I knew that. I knew what was his real vocation . . .'

They stood for a moment restively silent, embarrassed, like a group of people on Armistice Day. Then Seton wriggled his shoulders. 'Parson Dobson's getting married,' he said, in his normal voice. 'Quite by mistake, it seems. I must tell you all. A most fantastic story . . .'

Mrs Kennet let the conversation glide on ahead of her. Then, smiling gently, she joined in.

Even Seton didn't stay for dinner. That, for the moment, he felt, would have been going too far. When she had seen the last of her guests out of the house, Mrs Kennet closed the front door for the first time that evening. Then she turned the light off in the hall. She went back into the drawing room and stood by the fire, stretching out her hands to warm them; they were long, thin hands, so thin that the light of the fire almost seemed to be visible through them. She felt cold and unexpectedly lonely. Somewhere in the depths of the house, Sophy was cooking a meal. Behind her, she felt the darkened drawing room to be vast, unfamiliar, peopled by changing shadows.

When she heard the front door opened with a key, she stiffened, but did not move. She was afraid. Someone walked heavily down the hall and opened the door. She could not turn round. She heard the door shut, and knew that he was in the room. She didn't speak, because she could not control her voice. She waited, terrified, until his hands fell on her shoulders and turned her round.

'Kit.'

'I'm sorry I'm so late.'

He looked older by ten years. He had his overcoat on, and in it looked strangely broad and massive. He was half smiling. For the first time, she saw that he looked like Kennet.

'What do you want?' It was strange that she, who always wanted to see him, should ask him this as though she hated him.

'I wanted to talk to you.'

'What about?'

'About him. His death.' He paused a moment. She knew

that he was looking at her, searchingly, but could not bring herself to meet his eyes. 'I killed him.'

Her hands leapt to her throat, then fell again to her sides. 'Kit,' she said, 'don't ever say such a thing. Don't say it, Kit. Even to yourself.'

'I went away,' Kit said, 'before it happened. I didn't come back until afterwards. I've finished the work he left me. Now I'm here.'

'You're here.' She sat down on the sofa in front of him, her voice was lifeless, without feeling. 'They know who killed him.'

There was a short silence and then, relentlessly, he said, 'I'm going to tell you the whole story. You must know it. I shall tell you exactly what happened . . .'

When he had finished, she looked at him for the first time. He had not confided in her; he had simply told her the truth. She could think of nothing to say, and was still afraid. He was very gentle, and this frightened her. She could understand nothing. She was bewildered. At last she asked him, 'What are you going to do?'

His answer was incomprehensible to her. There was nothing to do but live with it, because there was no alternative. There was nowhere to go to, no release, no escape, no hiding place. He could try to make a new life, but in the end the new life would turn out to be the old one and he had to live it out. All the treachery, the guilt, the death was in him alone and in the past he had to look back on. Living, as Kennet had believed, was the only remedy. And yet Kennet had been killed.

She clasped her hands, like an old woman, on her lap. She could only ask, hesitantly. 'Have you had anything to eat? Will you stay?'

'No. No, I won't stay.'

She was relieved and yet, automatically, insisted, 'Are you sure? Are you sure you'll be all right, Kit?'

'I'll be all right.'

'I think I shall take a sleeping pill and get an early night. If you're quite sure . . .'

'I should do that. I wanted to tell you. Good-night.'

'Good-night, Kit. Good-night.'

She heard him walking away, the door closing. She was alone again and slowly, almost furtively, she leant back on the cushions. Her face was warmed by the dying firelight and a great feeling of relief came over her. Never again, she knew, would anyone interfere with her image of her husband and her son. She was free, now, to think of them as she thought they had once been; free to shape them into the men she had hoped, long ago, that they would be. The reality of them was too much for her. She could now create them again, differently, as her hands, held out to the fire, created two similar but indistinct shadows. She was no longer lonely.

As Kit walked away from the house, he brought his thoughts back to face the past as you bring round a horse's head for an impossible jump. As he had often done lately, he tried to remind himself of the pleasure Kennet had found in his last love affair, the coldness he had met in his marriage, the loneliness out of which he had continued to do what he expected of himself. He made himself think of the night he had met his father with Sylvia, as well as the night when he had woken up in a strange room and had decided not to telephone Katz. He made himself think of the exhaustion and the anger with which Kennet must have faced Katz at the end.

It was not true that it should have been himself, Kit, who had died. He was alive, and life was his only choice. Neither was it true that he was returning, at last, to his father's image. The present is the enemy of the past and fights it endlessly. Perhaps it was true that Kit, who had started by a violent, aimless attack on existence and had gone on to run away from it, was now coming towards it for the first time with the weight of all that he had done upon him, steadily, and only moderately afraid.

And it was true that as he walked down the shadowed pavement of a London street that evening in early summer, he looked more than ever before like the Kennet who had died.

THE END

FOR THE BEST IN PAPERBACKS, LOOK FOR THE 🐧

In every corner of the world, on every subject under the sun, Penguin represents quality and variety – the very best in publishing today.

For complete information about books available from Penguin – including Pelicans, Puffins, Peregrines and Penguin Classics – and how to order them, write to us at the appropriate address below. Please note that for copyright reasons the selection of books varies from country to country.

In the United Kingdom: For a complete list of books available from Penguin in the U.K., please write to *Dept E.P., Penguin Books Ltd, Harmondsworth, Middlesex, UB7 0DA*

In the United States: For a complete list of books available from Penguin in the U.S., please write to *Dept BA, Penguin, 299 Murray Hill Parkway, East Rutherford, New Jersey 07073*

In Canada: For a complete list of books available from Penguin in Canada, please write to *Penguin Books Canada Ltd, 2801 John Street, Markham, Ontario L3R 1B4*

In Australia: For a complete list of books available from Penguin in Australia, please write to the *Marketing Department, Penguin Books Australia Ltd, P.O. Box 257, Ringwood, Victoria 3134*

In New Zealand: For a complete list of books available from Penguin in New Zealand, please write to the *Marketing Department, Penguin Books (NZ) Ltd, Private Bag, Takapuna, Auckland 9*

In India: For a complete list of books available from Penguin, please write to *Penguin Overseas Ltd, 706 Eros Apartments, 56 Nehru Place, New Delhi, 110019*

In Holland: For a complete list of books available from Penguin in Holland, please write to *Penguin Books Nederland B.V., Postbus 195, NL–1380AD Weesp, Netherlands*

In Germany: For a complete list of books available from Penguin, please write to *Penguin Books Ltd, Friedrichstrasse 10 – 12, D–6000 Frankfurt Main 1, Federal Republic of Germany*

In Spain: For a complete list of books available from Penguin in Spain, please write to *Longman Penguin España, Calle San Nicolas 15, E–28013 Madrid, Spain*

A CHOICE OF PENGUIN FICTION

The Ghost Writer Philip Roth

Philip Roth's celebrated novel about a young writer who meets and falls in love with Anne Frank in New England – or so he thinks. 'Brilliant, witty and extremely elegant' – *Guardian*

Small World David Lodge

Shortlisted for the 1984 Booker Prize, *Small World* brings back Philip Swallow and Maurice Zapp for a jet-propelled journey into hilarity. 'The most brilliant and also the funniest novel that he has written' – *London Review of Books*

Treasures of Time Penelope Lively

Beautifully written, acutely observed, and filled with Penelope Lively's sharp but compassionate wit, *Treasures of Time* explores the relationship between the lives we live and the lives we think we live.

Absolute Beginners Colin MacInnes

The first 'teenage' novel, the classic of youth and disenchantment, *Absolute Beginners* is part of MacInnes's famous London trilogy – and now a brilliant film. 'MacInnes caught it first – and best' – *Harpers and Queen*

July's People Nadine Gordimer

Set in South Africa, this novel gives us an unforgettable look at the terrifying, tacit understanding and misunderstandings between blacks and whites. 'This is the best novel that Miss Gordimer has ever written' – Alan Paton in the *Saturday Review*

The Ice Age Margaret Drabble

'A continuously readable, continuously surprising book . . . here is a novelist who is not only popular and successful but formidably growing towards real stature' – *Observer*

A CHOICE OF PENGUIN FICTION

The Enigma of Arrival V. S. Naipaul

'For sheer abundance of talent, there can hardly be a writer alive who surpasses V. S. Naipaul. Whatever we may want in a novelist is to be found in his books . . .' Irving Howe in *The New York Times Book Review*. 'Naipaul is always brilliant' – Anthony Burgess in the *Observer*

Only Children Alison Lurie

When the Hubbards and the Zimmerns go to visit Anna on her idyllic farm, it becomes increasingly difficult to tell which are the adults, and which the children. 'It demands to be read' – *Financial Times*. 'There quite simply is no better living writer' – John Braine

My Family and Other Animals Gerald Durrell

Gerald Durrell's wonderfully comic account of his childhood years on Corfu and his development as a naturalist and zoologist. Soaked in Greek sunshine, it is a 'bewitching book' – *Sunday Times*

Getting it Right Elizabeth Jane Howard

A hairdresser in the West End, Gavin is sensitive, shy, into the arts, prone to spots and, at thirty-one, a virgin. He's a classic late developer – and maybe it's getting too late to develop at all? 'Crammed with incidental pleasures . . . sometimes sad but more frequently hilarious . . . *Getting it Right* gets it, comically, right' – Paul Bailey in the *London Standard*

The Vivisector Patrick White

In this prodigious novel about the life and death of a great painter, Patrick White, winner of the Nobel Prize for Literature, illuminates creative experience with unique truthfulness. 'One of the most interesting and absorbing novelists writing in English today' – Angus Wilson in the *Observer*

The Echoing Grove Rosamund Lehmann

'No English writer has told of the pains of women in love more truly or more movingly than Rosamund Lehmann' – Marghanita Laski 'She uses words with the enjoyment and mastery with which Renoir used paint' – Rebecca West in the *Sunday Times*. 'A magnificent achievement' – John Connell in the *Evening News*